4110

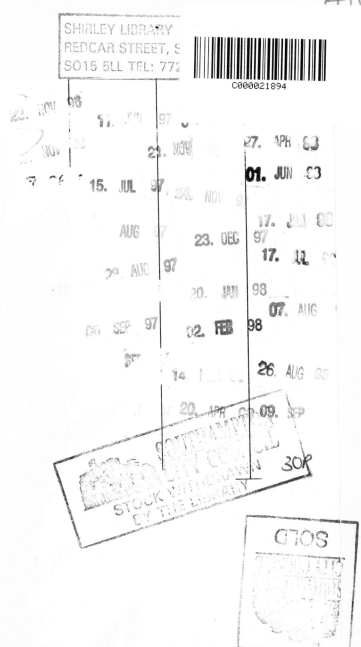

The Sinister Side

LUCILLA ANDREWS

The Sinister Side

HEINEMANN : LONDON

First published in Great Britain 1996
by William Heinemann Ltd
an imprint of Reed International Books Ltd
Michelin House, 81 Fulham Road, London SW3 6RB
and Auckland, Melbourne, Singapore and Toronto

A CIP catalogue record for this title
is available from the British Library
ISBN 0 434 00260 7

Typeset by Deltatype Ltd, Birkenhead, Merseyside
Printed and bound
by Clays Ltd, St Ives plc

ONE

MARIA WAS IN HER CASSANDRA MOOD THAT EVENING
so she wore her hair down, lashings of eyeshadow, no
lipstick, a sleeveless white linen shift and thonged san-
dals. She ignored the five nightingales singing in chorus
with the distant voices rehearsing 'The Silver Swan' and
fed me coffee, digestive biscuits and doom in the front
garden of her house on Littlehythe hill. The garden was
so crammed with golden forsythia, purple and white
lilacs, pink flowering-currants and banks of lavender
that no weed had a hope of survival. Nor, according to
Maria, had one of her neighbours.

'I just know it, Rose! I just know it! Max Jones last
Friday. The old Mercer woman, Monday. And this –' she
gestured wildly but having good reflexes caught the
coffee-pot in time – 'is Thursday! I just know there'll be
another in Littlehythe. I can sense something terrible's
going to happen and I'm terribly sensitive to atmospheres
– as you should know!'

She was dead right I should. Since she married Henry

Gillon three years ago in 1966 and discovered his mother, Lady Gillon, and my long late paternal grandmother had been cousins, she had decided I was the one member of 'the family' to whom she could really talk. She was a great talker and on her own admission so incapable of lifting a receiver without hearing heavy breathing or pottering down the hill to post a letter in the box outside her mother-in-law's house without narrowly escaping rape, murder, or both, that she made me feel inadequate and deprived. It was over four years since anyone had tried to murder me and in the interval I had only had one near-miss of accidental death.

The nightingales were singing in the Gillons' orchard that flanked their property on the upper hillside and was a sea of pink blossom; the human singers had moved on to 'Now is the Month of Maying'; and the half-moon was gently brightening in the clear, wide, powder-blue, country sky. It was the kind of late May evening for thinking beautiful thoughts and I could have done with a few after the strained drive up from the marsh. It had been strained as I had given a lift to Duncan Morgan, the founder, conductor and countertenor of the amateur Morgan Consort of Voices that on Thursday evenings practised in Lady Gillon's music room. Duncan had been Max Jones's host for the past year, arguably his only friend, and found that Max had died in his sleep when he took in his early tea on Saturday morning.

I reminded Maria that Duncan lived in St Martin's, a marsh village twenty-three miles from Littlehythe – which was too small even to rate as a hamlet. 'Max wasn't one of your neighbours and as he was fifty-three, grossly overweight, a heavy eater, smoker and boozer, he was asking for a fatal coronary, if that's what it was. Yes, like poor old Ginny Mercer's, his death was sudden, but you can't honestly say it was unexpected. In fact –' I gestured down the hill – 'as she had lived in the only cottage on Littlemarsh for over forty years and rode her aged bike up and down the marsh lane that's lined by a main dyke at all hours, in all weathers, it's a miracle she hit seventy-five before riding into it in Monday evening's mist. If it was as thick up here as round Endel, she couldn't have seen two foot ahead.'

She said mournfully, 'That's what Henry says. He rather liked her. So did Mama' (her chosen term for her mother-in-law, to the latter's irritation, since the Edwardian connotation reminded her she was old enough to be Maria's grandmother. She insisted I call her Maud). 'I've never understood why. That rude, bloody-minded old bat gave me the creeps. But Henry says if the coroner gives the go-ahead tomorrow, we must take Mama to the funeral on Saturday morning.' She waved tragically at the small, grey stone, eighteenth-century church directly across the lane that was still called 'the new St Mary's' as in Coxden, a village three miles from Littlehythe, was the St Mary's the Normans had built to replace the wooden church burnt down by the Danes in the tenth century. 'Cast a hideous blot on my birthday party.'

She would be twenty-eight on Saturday and was a few months older than me but suddenly, as so often, she made me feel as old as St Mary's, Coxden. She came from the Surrey stockbroker belt and after leaving her expensive girls' boarding-school with two Grade C O levels, spent a year in a Swiss finishing school, then lived at home 'doing lots of jolly jobs with horses and dogs and things' until she married. She was as untouched by the Swinging Sixties as the majority of her friends and

3

neighbours in rural Kent, and having married a man nineteen years her senior, remained as excited by birthdays and parties as the teenager she acted when Henry was around.

'Rubbish! Kent loves a good wake. Old Ginny wasn't everyone's pin-up, but as she'd been part of the scene for generations all first glasses will be knocked back to her memory and held out for seconds. What better way of getting any party off the ground?' I thought a moment. 'I think that would have amused her. She had a dry sense of humour.'

'I never saw any sign of it. I never even saw her smile. Actually, Mama got quite stroppy when I said that this morning. She said the poor soul had had a hard life and little cause for smiling and that when she was a gel – you know how Mama talks – she was a very pretty chubby blonde and your grandmother always said she was the best nursery-maid she'd ever had and was very sorry to lose her.'

I was surprised. 'She never told me she had worked in Endel.'

'Natch, not.' Maria nibbled another biscuit. 'Mama said this was ages before the uncle that left her Ferry Cottage and a small annuity died. She left Endel in the first war to marry some London chap but he was killed in France a day or two before he was due for leave, so she went into service in London. Inheriting Ferry bumped her up a bit. Natch, she wouldn't want to remind people she'd been a servant.'

'I guess not. Poor old Ginny,' I said sadly, thinking of the hatchet-faced, bitter-tongued old countrywoman who had always been uncharacteristically civil to me, purely, I suspected, because she had liked my father. His name had been Rosser Endel and at twenty-one he had left his parental home Endel House for good and never again contacted his widower father and elder brother. He had been killed in the second world war before I was old enough to remember him. Ginny Mercer had never forgotten him. 'Pick of the Endel crop was young Mr Rosser. Shame he never had a lad, but I'm glad the Lord saw fit for Endel to come to his girl . . .'

I had never known my paternal grandparents. My grandmother had died in a hunting accident when my father was fourteen and I had heard enough about her to be sorry I missed her. I did not regret missing my grandfather, of whom I had heard – and discovered – far more and, in consequence, locked his shade with those of his elder son and only grandson in a mental cupboard labelled UNDETECTED ENDEL MURDERERS. Their names had been respectively, Robert, Richard and Robert. For generations, all born Endels had Christian names beginning with R. I was the fifteenth, and as we all came from a long line of land-grabbers, profiteers, smugglers and, not coincidentally, farmers, I thought it highly probable my known trio were short of standing room.

I had first locked that cupboard just over four years back, on the icy February night that my cousin Robert's second attempt to murder me failed. First time, he had used an overturning tractor; second time he tried to drown me in a main dyke on Midstreet Marsh a few yards from the gates of Endel House. A generation earlier my grandfather and uncle had tried to drown my father in that same dyke and succeeded in murdering the friend with him on that occasion. The coroner's verdict had been 'Death by misadventure'. The Endels had always known how to cover their mistakes and close mouths.

My hair was still wet with dyke-water when I had been stunned to discover that as the last living born Endel I inherited the entailed estate. From then onwards, when others or circumstances forced the lock of my UEM cupboard I changed the subject.

I said, 'If it's on Saturday morning, I'll come up.'

'Mama said you would. When's Max's?'

'Coroner permitting, St Martin's, Monday morning.'

She peered into the entrails of the coffee-pot. 'There'll be a third, and it'll be someone equally foul.'

'Come off it, Maria! Ginny Mercer wasn't foul. She was just a harmless old recluse.'

'Huh! You're only saying that because she was marsh. You marsh lot always stick up for each other. She was as creepy as that scrounging old soak Max Jones – and don't pretend you liked him! You couldn't! He was repulsive and such a liar that Henry says he's still no notion how he earned a living before he muscled in on Duncan: every time they met, Max had a different story.'

I smiled. 'But a damned good story.'

'Darling, don't be so revoltingly charitable. It's nauseating. So was Max. Everyone thought so.'

'Not everyone.' I looked at the black flying-fox wind vane on the nearest of the two white-coned oasthouses higher up the hill and thought of Duncan's face this evening. 'Duncan's grief-stricken.'

'Not enough to miss tonight's practice,' she retorted with the certainty of someone who has never known great grief.

Duncan was waiting for me outside his closed garden gate, clutching a bulging music satchel and his violin case. The Consort sang unaccompanied, but he always

6

played duets with Lady Gillon after their practice ended. He wore an alpaca jacket and pink shirt, but instead of his usual polka-dotted, a black bow-tie; and there was an expression of bleak desolation on his normally cheerful foxy face and for once his bushy hair did not seem prematurely white. He peered nervously into the back of my orange Ford Escort even though I had earlier assured him over the telephone that I would leave my Alsatian with my gardener and, knowing his antipathy to dogs extended to their hairs, had just vacuumed the whole inside of my car.

'Jody's with Murdo,' I called, drawing up.

'Bless you. Just deposit these in your boot. Unlocked – ? Rose, my dear, you think of everything.' He dealt with this and got in beside me. 'I do hope my plea for transport has not too inconvenienced you. So stupid of me to leave my Mini's lights on all night but . . . er . . .' he fiddled with the buckle of his safety-belt: 'one tends to be absent-minded after – er – and I must thank you so much for your kind letter about – er . . .'

'I know, Duncan. You can't talk about him yet.'

He looked up tearfully. 'You're so young to understand. Of course – your husband – wasn't it a car crash?'

'Plane. Five years ago. All long over – and you're not inconveniencing me at all. It's a lovely evening for driving and for once I've spare time as our latest batch of kids have had to cancel because four have mumps.'

'No! Why's no one told me?' he demanded almost eagerly. He loved gossip, liked and was good with children, and took an active interest in the parties of disabled five-to-fourteens that, with their skilled attendants in rotation, used Endel as a holiday home from early May to late September. He had been a schoolteacher in the north of England until just after his fiftieth birthday he won a football pool and retired. He once told me that having no domestic ties he had spent a few months looking round England for he knew not what until he saw his present cottage. 'No near neighbours to object to my music-making and ideally placed for one with my passion for ornithology.' And being a quietly friendly man who willingly offered but never pressed his help on his neighbours and paid his bills by return, he had achieved a rare degree of local popularity for any incomer to a close-knit rural community that still clung to its traditional distrust of foreigners and included in this category the English without at least one marsh-born parent.

When he moved into his cottage a little under four years ago, the damaged roof of Endel had been repaired and the first party of children arrived. Since then, at varying intervals every summer, he voluntarily organised impromptu concerts for the children and had them all singing and playing improvised instruments to their communal joy. Afterwards he had sherry with me in my self-contained ground-floor flat. On every New Year's Day he invited me to his one annual pre-lunch cocktail party where he offered potato crisps, cheese biscuits and quantities of good champagne. This arrangement suited us both since we had little in common, if not as little as he assumed. But as I had loved my husband when I married him, I could empathise with his grief now, even though when Charles died I had run out of tears.

Last summer Max Jones had come down to the marsh to spend a weekend with Duncan and stayed on. Duncan said Max was his oldest friend and he relished his company. The local tradesmen and the landlord of the

Crown in St Martin's said that was nice, seeing Mr Morgan picked up all his old mate's tabs. A few of his neighbours wondered how that quiet, tidy Mr Morgan could be doing with that loud-mouthed, scruffy Mr Jones, but the majority said it took all sorts and no accounting for tastes, was there? Duncan had never discussed Max's provenance with me, and since, like Henry Gillon, Max had given me a different version at each telling, I had no idea of the truth. It was only yesterday that from my farm manager Walt Ames – who had it from PC Parker, our local cop – that I heard Max had once had a short, childless marriage in the States, long lost touch with his divorced American wife, and left a will naming Duncan his next of kin and leaving him all he possessed. 'Which ain't much, seemly, madam, seeing he was of no fixed abode before Mr Morgan took him in.'

On the drive over the flat, green, dyke-slit miles of the marsh we talked mumps, music, and the Consort's forthcoming concert in Cliffhill on Saturday week. Cliffhill, a small, ancient town that had once been a Channel port, stood on the cliffs that marked the southern inland tip of the marsh and that had been part of the coastline up to the mid-fifteenth century when the tide went out for good, the marshmen dug more dykes and the grass and the sheep took over the rich reclaimed land. Early in the last century the marsh and mainland had been divided by the wide, twenty-five-mile long Marsh Ditch that ran from Cliffhill to Norharbour, a seaside town on the northern coastal tip of the marsh where it flowed into the sea like a young river.

We were crossing the Ditch by the narrow, humped-backed stone bridge into Coxden when Duncan said, 'I hope you won't find sitting around too tedious, Rose.'

I knew what he meant but waited until I had taken the sharp left turn out of the suddenly widening, chestnut-lined main street. 'It's all right, Duncan. I know you loathe an audience at practices. I'll call on Maria Gillon.'

'Bless you, my dear. But first you must meet my young people. They'll be enthralled to meet the elusive Rose Endel of Endel.'

'Not elusive. Just too busy for socialising. Walt's a marvellous manager but he loathes paperwork so I do it and the Min. of Ag. never stops piling it on. Walt says it'll be far worse if we join the Common Market. Think we will?'

'No interest either way.'

I glanced at his distraught face and dropped the subject.

That side turning from Coxden was a short-cut to Littlemarsh Lane, which was a narrow, unfenced, un-built-up strip of tarmac running alongside the main dyke on an arm of marsh that reached up into the mainland to roughly one-third of a mile beyond Littlehythe hill. On the southern side the arm was backed by the long lowish ridges of Wedden hill. Wedden village sprawled along the top of what had been an island until Littlemarsh was drained in the late seventeenth century. The then incumbent ferryman had lost his job, but his cottage had survived. It stood on a small man-made mound about a hundred yards from the foot of Littlehythe hill and was fronted by a cross-dyke with a small, rickety wooden bridge that looked as old as the brickwork and sharply slanted tiled roof of the isolated little building. The curtains were closed across the two small, low, front windows and the even smaller dormer window and in the bright evening sunshine the impression was of old eyes closed in sleep, or death. But Littlemarsh was vibrantly alive with newly shorn sheep grazing the vivid green grass, land-based clouds of lapwing, curlew and strutting magpies, moorhens scuttling over the sparkling topaz dyke water and the dyke banks fringed with green and orange ferns and wind-stunted willows trailing long green fingers.

Duncan stirred. 'Wasn't it just here that poor old woman drowned?' he asked.

'Bit back.' I jerked a thumb over my left shoulder. 'Walt Ames told me her bike was fished out by that last clump of willows but her body had drifted nearly a mile towards the Ditch. His Kevin was one of the two tractor drivers who spotted her bike, gave the alarm, then helped get her body out.'

'Young Kevin?' he queried sharply. 'What was that boy doing along here? He works for Matthews in Coxden.'

'That's why. Tom Matthews owns those two oasts on Littlehythe hill and the ten-acre hopgarden up top. Some of his fleet of tractors are always up and down Little-marsh, since this is the short-cut to Coxden.' As I spoke a tractor turned slowly out of the foot of the hill. 'Kevin up. I'll get on to the right verge to let him by.'

The black-haired deeply tanned young tractor driver had recognised us and waved wildly. I waved back and as the tractor chugged by Kevin Ames yelled, smiling, 'Thanks, Miss Rose! Hi, Mr Morgan! What's up with the Mini?'

Duncan shouted, 'Flat battery,' and twisting to watch the tractor through the rear window muttered, 'Would that one still retained the resilience and insensitivity of youth.'

I didn't know what to say to that and we finished the drive in silence.

Lady Gillon had bought Potts' House, the only building at the foot of Littlehythe hill, after her husband's death thirty years ago. Potts, an eighteenth-century wool merchant and the first owner of the large, half-timbered house, had made his money from more than wool: from the small round smuggler's window set high in the east wall that faced the marsh. Above the window was the old, rusted, iron hook for the lantern hung out on nights when there were no Excise men around. The order was simple. No light: no deliveries. There was a smuggler's window in Endel and most other old houses on the marsh and this part of the mainland. The majority no longer served their original purposes.

Lady Gillon limped briskly down her paved front path as I drew up at the smaller of her two front gates. She was tall, thin, blue-haired and despite chronic angina and arthritic knees, still a strikingly well-preserved eighty-one and an accomplished amateur pianist. 'Why are you chauffeuring Duncan, Rose?' she demanded without preamble.

I explained, leapt out and stood on my toes for her customary peck on my left cheek. 'How are you, Maud?'

'As ever, flourishing. You're looking a bit washed out. Time you married again.' She offered a regal hand to Duncan. 'Tiresome about your car. So wise to come over. One must keep going. The others are putting their cars round the back.' She dismissed him to remove his possessions from my boot and ushered me up the path.

'You may sit in my drawing room or garden. We don't care for an audience in my music room.'

'Thanks, but I thought I'd go up to Maria. Is she in?'

'I can only presume so, as this is Henry's Rotary evening. We live our own lives. You may leave your car in my yard but before you deposit it there's something I've been wanting to ask you.' Duncan was back. She looked severely from him to me. 'Now what was it? Maddening how one keeps losing the thread in old age.'

Duncan nodded sympathetically. I mentally ground my teeth in anticipation of the inevitable, 'Have you accepted the Carmody boy yet and if not why not?' (Every man under forty was a 'boy' to Maud Gillon.) 'He's a personable boy of good stock and a competent young doctor, and that he lacks his father's brains is patently no disadvantage in your eyes since you have most ungratefully sent packing that clever Lofthouse boy who saved you from drowning a year or so back. But that's all water under the bridge and what matters is the future of Endel. Unless you re-marry and have children the entail dies with you. High time you remembered that!' I did. Nightly. And the murderous gene I refused to risk passing on.

'Ah! I have it. Maria says you loan Endel to these charitable institutions. Is she right?'

I smiled to hide my surprise on two counts. She had known this for years and I had never previously known her to forget anything even indirectly connected with the Gillons or the Endels. 'Yes.'

'You astonish me.' She turned to Duncan. 'My daughter-in-law is a charming gel and devoted little wife but so prone to hyperbole that I take all her pronouncements with dollops of salt. I owe her an apology.' She returned to me. 'As for you, child, were you not so visibly Rosser's daughter and possessed of several of his dear mother's mannerisms, I should now doubt your right to your inheritance. Your grandfather must be turning in his grave, but –' she smiled brilliantly – 'I approve. We must have another little talk later. Here come the others.' She beckoned to the five people filing round from the former stable-yard behind the house. 'Come along, my dears. Time to start.'

Duncan demurred deferentially. 'I'm sure they would like to meet Rose, Lady Gillon.'

'Very well. Come and meet my young kinswoman, Rose Endel,' she called to them.

The newcomers smiled politely. I smiled at the only one I knew more than by sight. He was a sturdy, fair, fresh-faced young man called Harry Todd and the best mechanic in the largest garage in Cliffhill. I recognised the thin, slight, dark-haired young man and his willowy ash-blonde wife as the youngish Londoners who last year had taken over one of Cliffhill's innumerable antique shops, and recalled someone telling me that the smallish, sexy twentyish brunette was a staff nurse at Cliffhill General Hospital and the balding, barrel-chested fortyish man, a solicitor's clerk.

Lady Gillon reeled off names and ignored Duncan's interpositions. 'Steven and Sandra Black –'

'Baritone and second soprano –'

'Christine Hicks –'

'First Soprano –'

'Frank Cross –'

'Bass –'

'And Harry Todd our tenor with whom I perceive you are well acquainted, Rose.'

While we exchanged brief pleasantries I also recognised from the way the Blacks and Christine Hicks were eyeing me that Duncan had already given them my tax bracket. During the past four years I had grown accustomed to this reaction in introductions, but it still made me writhe with guilt. Most psychiatrists would say this was responsible for my doing all the estate's secretarial work. They would probably be right, but only up to a point. Before I inherited Endel I had earned my own living as a secretary since I left school at seventeen, and frequently during my short marriage to a freelance writer I had been family breadwinner. I had never known and couldn't visualise adult life without a job and, irrespective of guilt, I enjoyed having one.

Maria found this incomprehensible. 'I can't think why you don't get a secretary. You'll have to when you re-marry. Henry says he wouldn't stand for my working, and most husbands feel the same.'

'Someone should remind them this is 1969, not 1869.'

'For God's sake, darling, don't remind Henry. He thinks the Sixties are a national disaster. What – ummm – does Julian Carmody think about you working?'

'No idea.' I glanced at my watch. The nightingales were singing unaccompanied. 'Doesn't sound as if they're playing duets tonight. I'd better get –' the ringing of the telephone in her front hall interrupted me. 'Probably Duncan for me.'

'Or one of *them*! Do wait!' She rushed in, leaving her front door open. 'Littlehythe 210 – oh! International? . . . Washington DC?' More than her excited voice had jerked me to my feet. 'Dr David Lofthouse calling person-to-person . . . No, I'm not Rose Endel but she's

15

here and I'll – oh, David! . . . Yes, Maria! . . . Yes, super, thanks! How are you? . . . Super! Yes, beside me – handing over now.' She thrust me the receiver and shot back to the garden, slamming the front door behind her.

Good or bad news? Could be either, I thought rapidly. 'Hi, David. Rose. How in hell did you know where to find me?'

He laughed. 'And it's great to hear you again, Rosie! Murdo. He says you're just fine. So am I, and as time's short just tell me straight if you're booked solid for the next ten days, as if not may I cadge bed-and-board from tomorrow night to Monday week?'

My upsurge of joy nearly throttled me. 'No – I mean yes, of course! How come?'

'My British boss wants me in London Monday week. My Yank boss says why don't I first take the short vacation back home. I thought I should call not cable in case you'd wedded another and forgotten to tell me.'

'Not me. How about you?'

'Not even once. You're sure this is all right with you, Rosie?'

There was so much I wanted to say and ask, but as we spoke the same language, one word was enough, 'Yes.'

'Thanks, love. Do I hire a car or can you meet the 5.25 from Astead in Coxden tomorrow evening?'

'Gladly. But why not Gatwick?'

'Business lunch in London first. All this only came up a few hours back. I'm flying tonight. Thanks again and see you Coxden tomorrow – and not one bloody minute before time.' The line went dead.

I replaced the receiver and dried my palms on the seat of my jeans. In the seven months since he had left to work in the States I had tried to kid myself I had my love for

16

him under control. Wrong there, I thought, but still right not to marry him. He hadn't thought so. We had fought fifteen rounds on that one. Was he coming back to go another fifteen – or for some other reason? What the hell! This time tomorrow he'll be back. I grinned euphorically and went back to Maria.

She had forgotten Cassandra, and her large, irregularly attractive face was alight with eager anticipation. She adored entertaining those she regarded as social top-of-the-pops and David's local reputation as a cross between Albert Einstein and the Brain of Britain, plus – despite Maud Gillon's views – the man most likely to collect the Endel jackpot, shot him to Number One on Saturday night.

'You must bring him, darling! Henry'll be dead chuffed – he actually likes David. He only pretends to like most of my friends as they make him feel old, poor sweetie, and he says he never knows what to say to them. He actually likes talking to David – only why's he in Washington? Why isn't he in Cape Whatever helping the Yanks put chaps on the moon?'

'God knows. I never ask about his work. He won't talk about it. He says he doesn't fancy a spell in the Scrubs.'

'Darling, you are so lucky! I wish Henry had signed the Official Secrets Act. Accountancy is yawn – yawn! Promise you'll bring him and we must fix up a cosy little dinner party later in the week – just a few special chums. Oh, poor Julian!' She flung her long hair on top of her head in delight. 'He'll sulk all Saturday night.'

I laughed. 'Having to stay on the wagon as this is his weekend on call won't help.'

'Darling, you're much more fun when you're bitchy. Must you go?'

I tilted my head to listen. The nightingales had stopped singing and there was no sound of distant music. 'I must. Duncan won't want to linger over Maud's coffee tonight. Thanks for yours.'

'Thanks for coming. It's been super.' She saw me to her garden gate. 'See you both Saturday night,' she added, too excited to remember she might see me that morning.

I was too euphoric to remind her. 'Sure. Give my love to Henry and –' but again her telephone started ringing.

'That'll be him saying he's starting back.' She rushed back to the house, forgetting the heavy breathers.

I drifted down the steep stone steps into the lane. The high banks on either side were carpeted with bluebells, buttercups, dandelions and fringed with white lace of cow parsley. The moonlight was brightening the gently darkening twilight, the soft warm air was scented with lilacs, lavender, new-mown hay and the rich damp soil of Littlemarsh. Somewhere close a solitary owl hooted. There was no traffic as I drifted on down the middle of the lane in a halcyon daze for another couple of minutes.

I was a few feet from Lady Gillon's front hedge when I heard someone running from her front door. Then Sandra Black catapulted through the smaller gate, her frightened face white and longish hair silvery in the moonlight. She rushed at me gasping, 'Duncan says you must go back and tell her – you know her – we don't – he's shattered – managed to ring her –' She began shaking violently and through chattering teeth mumbled, 'I always panic –' and couldn't say more.

I grabbed her narrow shoulders. 'Take a deep breath, Sandra, and start again.' She just stared as if I were a ghost. 'What's happened? Lady Gillon had another anginal attack? Is that what you want me to tell Maria

Gillon?' She winced, squeezed shut her eyes and I froze inwardly. 'Dead? Heart attack?'

That got through. 'How would I know?' she retorted frantically. 'I'm not a nurse like Chrissie. She – she had just sat down at the piano – keeled over – all the keys jangled. It was frightful – terrifying! Steve and Chrissie got her on the floor – Chrissie tried to get her breathing and shouted to Duncan to get an ambulance. She and Steve took turns kiss-of-life – you know – Frank and Harry were coping with the old maid – rushed in from the kitchen – hysterical – I just panicked – always do – hopeless with sick people.' She had to stop to gulp in breath. 'Duncan thought he should ring you first as you'd know what to do – only you'd gone so he had to talk to Mrs Gillon but couldn't bear to say – you know – so he just said taken ill. Mrs Gillon said she must ring her doctor first –' she wrenched off my hands. 'You must go back to her!'

I was numb with shock and about to say I must first see for myself that Lady Gillon was dead, but had no time. Maria was running down the hill. Sandra vanished and as I turned to face Maria racing towards me, her hair streaming out behind her and sandal-soles flapping on the macadam, a white barn owl with a struggling fieldmouse in its beak flew low across the lane between us. When in shock I invariably noticed trivial details and in that split second my mind flashed the thought – nature has no mercy, either. In the next second I had forgotten my instinctive reaction to the predatory owl and didn't recall it until the following evening in Coxden station yard when David handed me the mothball he had just found in the boot of my Ford. At that moment I had no idea why my mind had made that particular association.

It was later that I recognised that it took an Endel to think like an Endel.

TWO

DAVID WAS STILL SLEEPING OFF JETLAG IN MY SPARE bedroom when I left for Ginny Mercer's funeral next morning. All I had told him last night was that I had to go to one and would probably be back before he woke. He needed to catch up on sleep before taking on the ghosts.

At both of yesterday's inquests the verdict had been 'Death by misadventure'. In February four years back, yesterday's coroner had given the same verdict at the inquests on the deaths of my cousin Robert, his wife and brother-in-law. Their bodies had been dug out of the rubble after the roof caved in on the front hall and area of basement immediately below. No one but David and I had known that only Robert's wife, June, had been killed by the fall and that within the previous twenty minutes, Robert had murdered his brother-in-law and been accidentally killed by the mentally deranged June a few minutes before she intentionally tried to kill David. She would have succeeded had I not managed to lug David's unconscious body out on to the front porch and topple him down the steps just before the roof gave. Amongst all else the roof had buried was the secret of Robert's illegitimacy – his motive for needing me dead – and since none of it had any longer been relevant, David and I had kept it between us.

Marlene, who 'did' my flat, ushered me out through the side door into the front hall of the main house where Daph, her opposite number, promptly switched off the floor polisher. They eyed my black linen, three-quarter-sleeved button-through with covert approval – the marsh liked mourners to look like mourners – and sighed over the gift-wrapped packet in my hands.

'Shame poor Mrs Gillon had to cancel her birthday party.' Marlene, a statuesque blonde needing only the breastplate and horned helmet to double as Brünnhilde, folded her arms across her ample bosom. 'But not right to do no other after her poor ladyship gone sudden – rest her soul. They're saying up the village no inquest, like, seeing her ladyship's poorly heart had her under the doctor more years than we've had hot dinners.'

' "Natural causes", that's what, Marl.' Daph, small and sharply pretty, pulled off a plastic glove to pat her tightly home-permed black curls. They came out from St Martin's, the nearest village to Endel, six mornings a week, were friends since childhood now in their early thirties, married to Endel farm-workers, and Daph was the brains to Marlene's brawn. 'That's right, isn't it, Miss Rose?'

'Yes. Old Dr Carmody told me yesterday.'

That satisfied them as it had me. Dr Carmody senior was another of my father's boyhood friends, and to all his patients, a medical oracle.

They spent a couple of minutes agreeing it was nice for

poor Mr and Mrs Gillon to be spared all the talk in court, the papers, and local telly news. I spent the time looking round the long, narrowish, low-ceilinged, oak-panelled and floored hall that had an open hearth wide enough to burn a young tree and an impressive oak staircase running up from the back. It had been so well repaired that it was difficult to believe it had once been a triple tomb, but as it had I preferred to avoid the hall when the house was empty.

The conversation had moved on to the inquests. 'They're all saying as that Mr Morgan took on shocking up court, Miss Rose.' (For reasons of their own, like most of their neighbours they addressed me as the daughter of the house I had never been and had forgotten my married name long before I reverted to my own by deed poll this January. David's reaction had come in one line on a postcard: 'Do I reach for the Scotch or hemlock? D.')

I chose my words. Telling Marlene or Daph told St Martin's and half the marsh. 'Mr Jones was his old friend, Marlene.'

She nodded tolerantly. 'Takes all sorts.'

Daph sniffed, 'I'm not saying it don't but for all it's not right to speak poorly of them as gone, I reckon when Mr Morgan dries his tears he can count hisself best off. Nasty mouth in the drink had that Mr Jones – and hollow legs he had – and no saying he hadn't.' She paused belligerently, but neither of us contradicted her. 'Mark you, seeing he was well-spoken and had proper college schooling, he should've known better than to put back his sleeping tablets with the whole bottle of whisky for a nightcap, police doctor told coroner.'

'Still, he were a foreigner –' Marlene charitably left her sentence unfinished.

23

Daph hadn't finished. 'That old – umm – old Gin Mercer weren't no foreigner. Born St Martin's same as us, she was. She should've known better than to get back on her bike after Monday's WI supper-do up Coxden. Said in court and the papers you couldn't see your nose on your face up Littlemarsh same as down here.' Her mouth tightened. 'Some don't learn and won't be told. She was one.'

'That she was,' said Marlene and they exchanged a glance that hardened their good-natured faces.

I was only momentarily surprised by their uncharacteristic lack of charity for Ginny Mercer. The marsh generally forgave its own after death, but she had had a bitter tongue and the marsh had a long memory. Mine was in such good shape that I had to go out of the hall. 'Sorry, must go or be late.'

They saw me out to the front porch that faced the sea just under a mile to the south-east. Endel had been built on a large, man-made mound on Midstreet Marsh that was edged by the high, thick, concrete, sandbag-backed sea wall. When the sea broke through and swept away Midstreet village in the early sixteenth century only Endel and the village church another mile inland had survived. This morning the sea was at peace with the land and the incoming tide murmured over the broad swathe of pebbles that lapped the Midstreet Wall. And in the bright sunshine the sprawling, half-timbered old house looked strong enough to survive another four centuries. The great patches of new brown tiles on the massive, overhanging roof stood out as sharply as the fine seams of scars on David's chest and back after a hot bath. Those scars were the fundamental reason why I was alive.

Five years ago David had been severely burnt in an industrial accident and after six months in hospital he'd been medically advised to spend another six convalescing in clean air and quiet surroundings. He had seen an advertisement in a Sunday newspaper that had aroused his memory of an event in his childhood that his mother had always refused to discuss. The advertisement concerned End Cottage, which lay just outside the main gates of Endel and which my cousin rented furnished to holiday visitors. The event had been the accidental death by drowning of one of David's Scottish mother's two brothers, a young locum GP who had come down to the marsh at the suggestion of his great friend at Cambridge, Rosser Endel. David had taken End for six months and never mentioned his relationship to his long-dead uncle to anyone but me, and then only after he had risked his life to save mine. We had first met in the penultimate month of his tenancy, and initially his physical resemblance to Charles had made me dislike and distrust, and at times be terrified, of him. It was three weeks later that in the icy blackness of the dyke water I first saw him clearly. Less than a couple of hours after that recognition I lugged his unconscious figure out of the hall and toppled him down the front steps.

I glanced at the small, dyke-encircled cottage just beyond the always open gates as I went down the steps, then round to the old stables-yard behind the house. Between the world wars my grandfather had the stables converted to garages and a small flat built above for his married butler. The butler and nine resident female servants had vanished early in the second world war. During the winter months when the main part of the house was closed, it only needed the dailies, but to cater for the children, annually from mid-April to mid-October, I employed a resident cook and three maids. All four were at present away on an extra holiday consequent on the unexpected cancellation. I had offered the same time off to Marlene and Daph, but they had chosen to add it to the autumn holidays they took in rotation to coincide with their husbands' holidays. 'Can't have old Murdo doing without one of us to make his cuppa of a morning,' they said.

Murdo MacDonald, the gardener-cum-odd-job man, had occupied the stables flat for years. He was a small, scraggy Glaswegian who had come down to the marsh with his former employer in the late 1940s and after the latter's death was taken on by my grandfather. He was now over retirement age, but as he dreaded that prospect, was in good health, an inspired gardener, safe driver, loved dogs as much as he abhorred the majority of the human race but not children, whom he treated like puppies, and did his drinking in his own time off Endel land, I was happy to keep him on. He had got out my car and stood by it, chatting to Jody sitting upright on the back seat, her ears down and watchful eyes luminous with intelligence. She had been six weeks old when David had given her to me before leaving to work two years in the Australian branch of his firm British Chemicals Consolidated. She was now nearly four, a strong-boned, low-slung black-and-tan and, to those she trusted, a sheep in wolf's clothing.

Murdo fractionally raised the peak of his greasy tweed cap. 'Wee Jody's had a fine run.' He glared at my packet. 'You'll not be bearing gifts to the burying?'

'This is Mrs Gillon's birthday present.'

'Och, aye.' His crafty, wizened face creased dourly.

'It'll nae be one she'll wish to recall. Will Mr Lofthouse be keeping to his bed?'

'Still flat out. I'm just remembering,' I lied, 'that last night I forgot to tell him I'm going over to Mrs Gillon's after the funeral and may be back later than he expects. If he's up before your half-day, will you tell him?'

He gave the ambiguous grimace that was his equivalent of a smile. David was one of the rare people he liked. 'I'll inform him if he's about before I'm away out. I'm away up the house just now for my fly-cup and wee blether with the lasses.' He ambled off to the main kitchen at the back of the house. Only the upper windows at the back overlooked the yard. I got into the car and checked my reflection in the driving-mirror until he was out of sight. 'Just want to look in the boot, Jody. Wait. Back in a moment.'

It was more than a moment before I returned to the driving-seat and spent several more looking at the mothball I had found under the spare wheel. I had dropped the first in the litter-bin in Coxden yard yesterday. Now I wrapped the second in a face tissue and zipped it in my sling-handbag.

St Mary's, Littlehythe was still near-empty when Maria beckoned me to Henry's vicar's warden's pew. She wore her hair up in a french knot, and a long-sleeved black silk bolero over a cream shirtwaister; Henry's dark suit and black tie made him look longer and thinner than usual. Aside from Christine Hicks sitting alone two pews ahead in a trim, long-sleeved white blouse and black cotton miniskirt, the rest of the sparse congregation were elderly.

Maria stooped to whisper to me, 'She told us outside she nursed her last winter and got fond of her. Sweet of

27

her to come over, isn't it? We're terribly grateful to her. Dr Carmody told Henry no one could have done more for –' she was silenced by Henry's nudge. We all rose and from behind us the vicar began intoning, 'I am the resurrection and the life, saith the Lord . . .'

The old graveyard lay on the southern side of the church. Christine Hicks joined us when we trailed back to the lych-gate. She refused my offer of a lift back to Cliffhill. 'Thanks awfully, but no need to take you ten miles out of your way. The Saturdays-only 11.15 from Coxden passes the foot of this hill in ten minutes and stops outside the hospital.' The smile that dimpled her chubby cheeks was directed more at the Gillons than me. 'One of the things I love about working in the country is the way everyone's so kind about offering lifts.'

Henry said he was glad to hear it. Maria added with a hint of Maud Gillon's regality, 'If you can get off for my dear mother-in-law's funeral on Tuesday afternoon we hope you will come back to tea with us afterwards.'

Christine's smile vanished and her round brown eyes glowed with what, perhaps unfairly, struck me as practised compassion. 'Oh, thank you, Mrs Gillon. I've already fixed my off-duty with my ward sister. We're all coming.'

'Then you must come back to tea. My husband and I are so grateful to you all, and particularly to you.'

'I just wish I could have done more.' Christine glanced back at the little church. 'And I so wish more could have been done for poor Miss Mercer – but far too late for anything but regret. I was awfully upset when I heard she'd drowned. I got really fond of her when she came into my ward with bronchial pneumonia in February. She wasn't in long –' she smiled faintly, disarmingly –

'and I can't pretend she was an easy patient, but she was such a fighter. I love nursing the fighters.' She checked her watch. 'Do forgive me. Mustn't miss my bus.' She nodded a communal farewell and hurried purposefully downhill.

Henry looked after her. 'A very nice, competent girl.'

'An absolute sweetie!' Maria gushed girlishly, switching from *grande dame* to teenager to comfort him. 'Dr Carmody says the General is lucky to have her as she trained in one of the big London hospitals and it shows.'

It had on Thursday evening. Dr Carmody had had to come up from St Martin's and until he arrived Christine had taken charge with impressive efficiency and tact. She had told me she was twenty-four and needed another year's experience as a senior staff nurse before applying for a ward sister's post. I was sure she would get one, if that was what she really wanted, but I wouldn't have cared to be one of her juniors. She reminded me too much of a prefect in my second year in a girl's grammar school, who had been drooled over by the staff and regularly reduced first-years to tears of sorrow, and seconds, including myself, to tears of rage. She had gone on to Cambridge tipped as a certain first in Eng. Lit. and in her second year dropped out to marry one of her tutors who just happened to have a healthy private income. She had known how to use her talents to get what she really wanted, I reflected, paying lip-service to Maria's continuing eulogy. I wondered what Christine hoped to gain from this public demonstration of her affection for Ginny Mercer, then reminded myself funerals always made me bitchy and Maria's present was still in my car.

'Darling, super! You must come in for a sherry.'

It was another hour before I got back to Midstreet and

saw David standing on the sea wall. He waved me down and the joy of seeing him there was so overwhelming that I forgot to wave back. I turned off the coast road on to the private cinder road that was Endel property and stopped a few yards short of Endel Cottage. David came quickly down the steep concrete steps left clear of sandbags, then had to wait for three cars towing caravans to pass before crossing. He fitted the holiday visitors' picture. He wore dark glasses over his normal pair, a garishly multicoloured short-sleeved, open-necked shirt loose over fawn denims and his fair hair was as bleached and solid square-jawed face as tanned as when he returned from Australia last year. The American outfit suited his tallish, sturdy figure, but I could have done without the reminder of the width of the Atlantic. Jody, upright as a dowager on the back seat, thumped her tail. She never forgot a friend or a foe. 'You and me both, Jody,' I murmured, smiling at David crossing the road and refusing to think of the hell of Tuesday week. I leant over to unlock and open the front passenger door. 'All you need are the stars and stripes, David.'

He grinned. He had very good, and being a heavy smoker unfairly white, teeth. 'Statutory summer clobber for the all-American egghead, love.' He got in and after disentangling himself from Jody's welcome, asked, 'Security clearance kiss the lady, Jody?' Her tail hammered the back seat. 'Thanks, lass.' He took off both pairs of glasses and kissed me as wonderfully as always, but the tension in his arms was new. Ghosts back, I registered vaguely, 'Christ, but it's good to see you, Rosie and looking more than good in that elegant little number.' He replaced only his normal black-rimmed glasses. 'Like me to give her a run before lunch?'

'No need, thanks. New routine. You'll see.' Murdo must have been talking to him, I thought far less vaguely. Marlene and Daph were four-star gossips; Murdo rated five. I drove on through the open iron gates that no amount of repainting saved from re-rusting in the salty air and drew up some thirty yards on. 'She now thinks she's a carriage-dog and as this is a child-free Saturday with no staff but Murdo, and no delivery vans, sheep, geese or cats around, it's safe to indulge her.' I let Jody out, she raced round to the nearside mown grass verge and crouched to pace the car up the half-mile drive. 'Murdo tell you why I'm late back?' I asked unnecessarily.

'*Inter alia*. How was the funeral?'

'A funeral.'

'I'll bet.' He paused briefly. 'Two more scheduled. What's been going on down the marsh that you haven't told me?'

'Nothing that you haven't known years.' I drove on slowly. He had hitched down his glasses and was watching me over the tops as always when he wanted a clearer view of a close object. 'People have drowned in dykes since they were first dug, in drunken stupors since they did it on mead, and of heart failure in old age since God only knows when.'

'That's for sure. If I hadn't been so bloody pushed I would have remembered to pack a black tie.'

'You won't need one Monday if you can face coming with me. You will for Lady Gillon's, Tuesday afternoon and if you don't come Maria'll give me hell. She wants us back to tea. "Everyone is just longing to see David again, darling." '

He groaned. 'I'm not stopping. How soon can you run me to Gatwick?'

I glanced at his shirt. 'Why not Astead for the next fast to London?'

He hesitated. Then, 'Freudian slip. Unfinished business on my mind.'

I slowed the car more. Jody raced ahead then flopped triumphantly down by the old mounting-block a few feet left of the front steps. 'Anything you can tell me about?'

'Yes, but not right now. It's complex and I'm not yet wholly back in touch with reality.'

I stopped the car, switched off and faced him. His blue eyes met mine steadily and guardedly. 'Can't you just give me the punchline now?'

He looked towards End Cottage. 'My Yank boss wants me to stay in the team.'

I had no right to feel kicked in the stomach. I just did. 'But BCC don't want to lose you so the Chairman lunched you yesterday?'

He turned back to me. 'He's the good boss of a good organisation that's been bloody good to me. I'm keeping my options open until I've thought this through and talked it over with you. I like the States, the job and the mates I've made over there – but it's one hell of a haul from Endel. Let's leave it on the back burner and get in. I've some duty-free whisky I forgot to give you last night. Any beer in the joint?'

'A case of Newcastle Brown I got in for you yesterday.'

He laughed almost naturally, 'Do you wonder I keep coming back like a homing pigeon, Rosie?' He got out of the car quickly and went straight into another slop-session with Jody.

I got out slowly and looked up at Endel as if seeing it

for the first time. The front door was closed and bolted on the inside, as always when the house was left empty. All the domestic staff had their own main back-door keys and only Walt Ames the keys to the front door of my flat that had been set above the nine brick steps at the back to avoid spoiling the appearance of the front. Looking up at the house now I remembered how at first sight it had given me the impression of a great cat crouched to spring. It sprang and caught me in its paws for life, I thought, following David and Jody round to the back, but as it had given me so much I had no right to resent the price-tag. I resented passionately what it had cost David.

While we got lunch and for most of the meal, more than our unfinished conversation hung between us like an electric curtain. Last evening he had been so punch-drunk with the combination of jetlag and his boss's claret at lunch that he had been asleep before sunset. We made small-talk to which neither of us listened until I told him I had found a second mothball. 'Must have rolled out of Duncan's violin case. Only he and you have used the boot since I vacuumed it Thursday afternoon.'

'Why not? From the little I ever saw of him I'd have said he was a bloke to reach for his mothballs at the first flutter of a passing moth.'

'He would. Only I've never smelt them on the innumerable occasions that he's opened his case in my presence.'

He blinked at me thoughtfully. 'Maybe the moths only got at the lining very recently.'

'Yes. I expect that's it.'

He yelped with laughter. 'Like hell you do! One sniff of mothballs and you've slapped dope-runner on poor old Dunk.'

I coloured but was too accustomed to the rapidity of his insight to dissemble or remember how this once terrified me. 'Walt told me they sometimes use mothballs to disguise the smell.'

'Hell, Rosie,' he protested. 'That one had hairs on it when I was wandering round marsh pubs supping jars and chatting up the natives months before you blasted into my life like Apollo 10. As every marsh cop, coast-guard and Customs bloke'll have known it years, any blokes running it in must have long switched tactics. Much coming in this way?'

'Not that I've heard. When Walt told me this last year he said only occasionally. But something's always coming in.'

'In view of the fact that smuggling's been the priority part-time occupation for marshmen since they ferried the loot in their coracles, tell me something I don't know. Dunk's no marshman. Why make the connection? Word out on him?' I shook my head. 'So why?'

I shrugged, 'Primordial instincts, I guess.'

'Christ, no! No! If you're into another wallow in ancestral guilt I need a fag. Knock off that bloody Endel chip and say if you mind my smoking before the cheese.'

'Go ahead while I scrape the egg of my face.'

He was instantly contrite. 'Sorry, Rosie – let me.' He ran a forefinger gently down my left cheek. 'I've enough chips to fill in every bloody dyke on the marsh. High time I stopped cracking at yours. You're no more responsible for your genetic equipment than you are for your lovely face.' He lit up and for several seconds gazed out of the open dining-room window that was at the front of the house. A faint heat haze shimmered over the marsh and the sound of the traffic on the coast road was soft as the drone of a bee. 'Which football pool did he win?'

I blinked mentally. 'No idea. Think there's a connection?'

He looked at me. 'I think there's a high degree of probability that's as non-existent as the late Miss Mercer's long-lost bastard infant.'

'As *what*?' I was incredulous. 'Get this from Murdo?' He nodded. 'Who told him? Why's no one ever told me? Sooner or later I hear all the dirt.'

'Cool it. Ancient dirt.' He stubbed out the cigarette, then stood up to remove our plates to the serving hatch and bring the cheeseboard and biscuits from the sideboard. 'Murdo said she had the kid early in the first world war.'

'Good God, man, you've spent too long amongst our ex-colonists if you've forgotten fifty-odd years is yesterday to the marsh and still in some living memories. What exactly did he tell you and how did it come up?'

He sat down again. 'He had shown me the reports on the inquests in yesterday's *Astead Evening Gazette* and given me his unrepeatable opinion of Dunk's late-lamented, when he said you looked a wee bit down in the mouth this forenoon and it was right there should be one or two to mourn the poor old soul as to his way of thinking there'd not be many. I asked why not – and got the lot.' He stopped for thought. 'Did you know she once worked in Endel?'

My mind had gone into overdrive. 'Only from Maria just before your call. She was doing her Cassandra.' I told him what she had said and what had followed his call. I left out the owl. 'For once her vibes were right.' He nodded sombrely. 'She can't have heard about this baby or she'd have told me. She didn't like Ginny. She said she gave her the creeps. Go on with Murdo's version.'

'He said she'd left Endel with a good reference to work for some young war widow in Coxden with three small kids and a large house. He didn't know the name of the widow or the house. "Away afore ma time doon sooth, Mr Lofthouse." He said she then got pregnant, but that neither she, her parents, nor – and this makes me doubt the lot – her employer, ever admitted this, but when it became obvious she was packed off to relatives in London and a few months later returned slimmer and alone to her old job.' He looked at me and shook his head. 'I don't buy a respectable Edwardian widow taking what she would regard as a fallen woman back to look after her kids. But if Maria's got it right, it adds up. Having lost her husband she'd sympathise like hell with a girl who had just had her bloke killed in action.'

'Yes. Murdo didn't mention the dead soldier?'

'No.' He offered me the cheeseboard and when I shook my head looked at it meditatively but didn't take any. 'He said –' he switched into broad Glaswegian – 'It's aye been said it was some Coxden laddie that put her in the family way and she left others to fend for her wee wean. Nae forgiven and nae forgotten.'

'If she had a baby, he's right.' I stared unseeingly at the vase of yellow roses on the table that Murdo had begrudgingly cut yesterday. All I saw were the faces flicking through my mental vision; faces of the living and the dead. Marlene and Daph's this morning; Ginny Mercer's bitter old face juxtaposing with the imaginary face of a pretty, chubby blonde girl; then another face I had first seen in the portrait that had hung over the mantelpiece in the large drawing room across the front hall until I converted this to the children's playroom. That portrait of my grandfather in middle age had been rehung amongst the other old family portraits lining the walls of the second-floor corridor. All the born Endels had my black hair, brown eyes and pale complexions and the men had hard, handsome faces. 'This could be why there were so few at her funeral, and explain Marlene and Daph's bitchiness.' I looked up and saw he was watching me with the stolid expression that meant his hyper-analytical brain was pursuing a problem of its own. 'The marsh villages have been so isolated and inbred until roughly our lifetime that St Martin's still shrugs off adultery, fornication, even incest, as "Well, not right, mind – but folks will, won't they?" But the one unforgivable sin is for a woman to abandon her baby. May God forgive her. St Martin's won't. Ever.' I paused but he said nothing. 'Murdo know the father's name?'

' "I d'ya ken. Away afore ma time doon sooth." '

'Believe that?'

He smiled slightly. 'When did my nasty, suspicious mind believe anything I'm told without hard evidence to verify it?'

'But you always spot a liar. Was he lying?'

'I think he believed what he told me though I thought it very probably a load of old cobblers. Too many gaps. He didn't know the kid's sex, or even if it survived.'

I breathed out a little mentally. 'Perhaps it was stillborn.'

'Possibly. Equally possibly it survived, was raised by her London relatives or farmed out to others. No welfare state then. Families had to handle their own problems and some did that bloody well. I kid you not, Rosie,' he said firmly. 'Back where I come from either old Gran,

37

Aunty Kate or Cousin Minnie automatically took in the family by-blows. Some had it bloody tough. Others had it bloody nicely and have since done better. There are one hell of a lot worse fates for a bastard than being assimilated into a large, close-knit, impoverished, working-class family. And as her London relatives appear to have been willing to shelter the mother, it's a reasonable assumption they did the same for her baby.'

I gestured apologetically, 'I'd forgotten that still happens in St Martin's.'

'You're not a lad up from the working classes, love. Shall I get the coffee?'

'Thanks – oh – sorry. Forgot to switch it on.'

He stood up. 'I'll fix it and load your dishwasher.'

'Sorry again – it's bust. We don't know why. A mechanic from Cliffhill's coming to deal with it on Tuesday.'

'Like me to look at it?' His attention was attracted to a red motorbike roaring up the drive. 'Don't I know that Norton?'

'Yes. That's Kevin Ames under the helmet and goggles. He often gives Murdo a lift somewhere on Saturday afternoons and sometimes does odd-jobs in the garden when he's short of lolly.' Kevin had seen us and we exchanged waves as he shot on round to the yard. 'Murdo says he's nae so cackhanded with a hoe for a laddie too grrreen to burrrn.'

'He told me this morning.'

'You had some chat.'

'My old mate since End.' He leant on the back of his chair and looked at me quizzically. 'In this morning's update he threw in the Young Doctor's avid interest in the young mistress. Leading a packed field, he said. He thought I should know.'

'Oh, aye?' I mimicked. 'Anything I should know?'

'Nowt.' The expression in his eyes altered. 'I've tried like hell to get you out of my blood. No dice. Only you are you. Option still rests with you, so if you ever change your mind and ask me to wed you, any time'll suit – and don't forget you don't have to ask nicely.'

I knew now precisely why he had come back to Endel and how much depended upon my answer. I had to be honest – and not only because he would see through a lie. 'David, I haven't forgotten and I can't change my mind.' His face tensed. 'I wish to God that I could – this is so unfair to you and –'

'Stuff that! I told you from starters I'll settle for your terms. That's my decision, not yours. Like me to look at your dishwasher?'

I looked at him for a few moments. 'Thanks very much.'

He flushed and his knuckles whitened on the chair. 'I'll fix our coffee first.'

I stood up and held out a hand. 'Couldn't we have it later?'

He smiled slowly, gloriously, and held out his arms, 'I'm not thirsting for coffee, love.'

The percolator was still cold when my bedside telephone rang at 4.30. David smiled dreamily, disentangled an arm and passed me the receiver. I held it between our heads. 'Midstreet 17. Rose Endel.'

'Rose, my dear, Duncan here.' The light tenor voice was reproachful. 'I've only just heard our brilliant young physicist is back in our midst. Why haven't you told me the happy news?'

'I only heard he was coming at Maria's evening before last. It wasn't the right moment.'

'True, alas, so true. So much sorrow – how long is he with you? . . . May I venture to hope the dear boy will accompany you on Monday morning and that you will after come back here to drink a final toast to my dear Max? It will be such a comfort to have you both with us.'

'Thanks, Duncan, but as I'm not sure of David's plans, just hold a moment, please.' I covered the mouthpiece and, knowing David's acute hearing, said, 'The champagne'll be good.'

He scowled, took the receiver, spoke to Duncan for a couple of minutes, then put it down and drew me closer. 'The things I do for you, Rosie, bugger belief.'

'Just call you Galahad and have done.'

'Feel free.' He raised his head to look into my face. 'Why are Dunk and I now buddy-buddies? On past showing we have a problem getting beyond the first how-do.'

I smiled dreamily. 'I expect he wants his mothballs back.' And we laughed as if I had made the joke of the year.

I hadn't.

THREE

'THIS HAS THE MAKINGS OF ANOTHER BLOODY GOOD wake.' David sipped champagne and took a comprehensive look around the crowded rose-garden behind the Gillons' house. 'Who are we seeing off tomorrow, Rosie?'

I kicked his ankle and smiled high over his head. 'Good afternoon, General.'

'Afternoon, m'dear – Lofthouse.' General Wenden's towering figure edged between us. He had been a lifelong friend of Lady Gillon, a boyhood friend of my father and his rigid old soldier's face was firmly cheerful. The funeral was over and it was time to rally the troops' morale. 'Great loss, Maud Gillon. Fine woman. Had a good innings and went in action. Can't ask for more. Hmmm. Heard you're back on a spot of leave, Lofthouse. If you'll forgive us m'dear –' he drew David aside. 'They tell me you've been working for NASA. Did you run across one of my former junior officers – chap called . . .'

41

I knew my place in the general's world and backed away. He had been a widower for years, had no daughters and as his two married sons lived and worked at opposite sides of the world, he regarded young women as a delicate, unpredictable species incapable of discussing anything but trivia. From other men that attitude infuriated me, but as I liked him enormously, it amused me. I smiled at Maria across rosebeds. She flashed back her *grande dame* smile and a hovering waitress offered me minuscule cucumber sandwiches and miniature chocolate éclairs.

The posse of hired waitresses began circulating the champagne immediately the first 'chosen' mourners trailed over from the lych-gate. Maria led the trail; Henry rounded up the stragglers like a weary, spidery, sheepdog. Henry had aged years in days. Maria looked younger and despite her reddened eyes, glowed with a new self-assurance that reminded me that even the saddest death brings a measure of release. She had a new black sombrero, black and white silk two-piece and long black gloves. She shed the gloves directly she was through her front gate, and the champagne removed the solemnity from her guests' faces nearly as swiftly.

'Just a few special chums, darling.' For the first time she stooped to peck my cheek and just missed knocking off both our hats. (Mine was a small black straw boater, since, being five foot three, anything larger made me look a walking standard lamp.) 'Super to see you, David. Just wish it could have been a happier occasion.' Her eyes brightened at the unusual elegance of his well-cut, lightweight grey suit, white silk shirt and the black tie that, with my hat, we had bought in Cliffhill early yesterday morning. 'You look super! Poor darling Mama would have been so chuffed. She always said no hostess could ever have too many attractive men,' she added artlessly, beckoning a champagne-laden waitress. 'Long cosy chat anon – do forgive me.' She sailed off to attend other arrivals.

'Oh, Miss Rose, I never thought to see this day!' Old Nora, Lady Gillon's maid, in her best Sunday black, backed me further from General Wenden and David. 'Always thought I'd be took first and never wanted no other.' She mopped her eyes and gulped champagne. 'Fifty-nine years I been with her ladyship – oh, no, ta, dear, I don't think I should – oh, well if you say so, Miss Rose, just the drop, ta –' She accepted the refill from a napkin-wrapped bottle. 'Oh, Miss Rose, I don't know what I'll do without her ladyship but Mr Henry's ever so kind and says I'm not to worry over nothing and leave it to him.'

'I'm glad but not surprised, Nora. He's so fond of you and you've always been a part of his life.'

The champagne was steadying her. She said with a resigned acceptance, 'No part for me in his new life, miss. Comes to us all.' Her faded but still sharp grey eyes looked backward. 'Lovely baby, he was. Lovely little lad and for all her ladyship had to wait the ten years before he come and never had no more, the master made sure as he wasn't spoilt. Not that he wasn't real made up having a son, same as her ladyship. Not easy for her it wasn't, seeing her young sister Miss Violet had the three. Mrs Jarvis she was and poor Major Jarvis killed first Christmas Day of the Great War – but you'll not want to hear all this.' She peered at my face. 'How you keeping, miss? Looking all eyes and like a good breath'll blow you away. Just like your poor father.'

43

It wasn't the moment to remind her I had weighed seven stones since I left school and my father had been a healthy twenty-five when his torpedoed corvette sank with all hands in mid-Atlantic in December 1943. I falsely blamed the hot weather and asked after her health.

'Just the rheumatics, miss, and can you wonder living so close Littlemarsh all these years.' She watched Henry Gillon remove David from General Wenden and Duncan, who had just joined them. 'Nice to see you got your young gentleman friend back with you. Be hearing wedding bells soon, will we? Nothing would have pleased her ladyship more. Time and again she said to me – oh, Mr Morgan!'

'Dear Nora.' Duncan clasped her hand in both of his and gave me a sad little smile. He was pink-faced and sweating in a too-tight dark suit that reeked of moth-balls. While he and Nora chatted I caught David's eye and brushed a forefinger down my left cheek. He smiled widely and then returned his attention to Major and Mrs Dawson, a retired couple that were Duncan's nearest neighbours and whom David had met yesterday.

When another of Lady Gillon's friends claimed Nora, Duncan and I withdrew and he told me he hadn't worn his suit since his last Founder's Day. 'My dear Max would have been appalled had one donned it yesterday. But our dear Lady Gillon was of the old school – need one say more? Ah!' A waitress offered tea in fluted bone china crockery. 'May I take one for you and dispense with your glass?'

'Please. I lost the toss; I'm driving.'

'You and the dear boy are so compatible. So many,

alas, are not. As indeed you cannot have failed to observe yesterday.'

I looked at him as if I had been far too dumb to notice in his cottage yesterday that it had taken the combined efforts of the Dawsons, Frank Cross, David and myself, to paper over the blazing row the Blacks were having in one corner and Christine and Harry in another. Last night David and I had agreed the trouble with the latter was that Christine was too bright for Harry and he too immature for her. We had disagreed over the Blacks. I thought Steven's rudeness to his wife rated all she handed him. David said that if *he* had been daft enough to wed that piece of poison ivy he would have been far ruder and would long have beaten it for the divorce courts. 'I wouldn't call her poison, David – just a thirtyish Ophelia.' 'Balls, love! Ophelia was a sweet, nutty kid. Our Sandra's no sweet kid –' he hesitated – 'and if she's a nutter I'm a fruitcake.'

I said to Duncan, 'We were all so distressed for you.'

'Dear Rose. So kind. And your dear boy is a veritable tower of strength. You are bringing him to our concert?'

'He's looking forward to it,' I lied enthusiastically. On Sunday morning when I warned David we would have to attend he had taken the dishwasher apart and put it back in working order before he stopped moaning.

'How one cherishes the support of one's friends.' Duncan peered over the surrounding backs. 'I didn't see the Chief Constable at the service, but isn't that his wife talking to David?'

'Probably. I can only see the back of his head but if she's short and solid in a matching grey silk toque and dress, it's Lady Hurst. She told us outside the church that Sir Norman had to be in Maidstone this afternoon.'

'One had heard he was at school with your father,' he murmured as if his mind was elsewhere. 'Oh dear – poor young Harry needs succour. A little out of his depth. Pray excuse me.' He drifted off into the crowd.

The faces grew redder, the voices louder; the portion of the crowd that had spilled into the orchard were sprinkled with pink blossom that looked like confetti and not inappropriate. The conversations had moved from 'Wonderful woman, Maud Gillon! Aren't Henry and Maria being wonderful!' which had temporarily united friends and foes. Now the assembled company split into little groups of kindred spirits and in my varying images I was sucked into one after another. As a landowner I talked farming with the farmers; as a war orphan I was warmly welcomed by the clique of retired officers from the three services re-fighting the second world war; and as a rich young widow I was the object of special interest to the several blue-haired ladies with unmarriageable or newly divorced sons. '. . . so fortunate divorce no longer carries the social stigma it had when I was your age, Rose. One had to ostracise the divorced or be ostracised oneself!' They enthused over David's return, insisted I bring him round for drinks, luncheon, dinner, as Jonathan, Nigel, Simon were just dying to meet him, and concealed their satisfaction that David was keeping upon me no more than the eye a considerate guest should on his hostess. 'When does he return to America? . . . What a pity it's such a short holiday!'

Harry Todd kept reappearing at my side. He was unrecognisably spruce in black jacket, grey slacks, white shirt and black tie loaned by his boss, George Ames, the elder of Walt's three younger brothers. Harry was due back at work at five and we commiserated with each other at being on the wagon.

'Tell you the truth, Mrs Endel, if I get back with the whiff on me breath the guv'll hand me me cards before I gets on me overalls.' Harry's candid boyish face smiled shyly. 'I reckon I'd have had 'em already for asking time off two working days running if he weren't your Mr Ames's brother. But Chrissie said if I didn't turn up I could find meself another bird. Not fair to poor old Duncan to chicken out, she said.' He scanned the garden. 'I dunno where she's hiding herself.'

'Tried the orchard?'

'Nah. Ta. I'll give it a go.'

'Rose, come and tell us how you feel about the Common Market.' Major Dawson drew me back amongst the ex-servicemen. 'Don't you think the Frogs are behaving disgracefully?'

An older man snorted, 'Where would they be now but for our chaps, eh?'

'With respect, Brigadier,' put in Julian Carmody's voice from behind me, 'do we really want to join the Frogs and other riff-raff over the water? If our lamentable Labour government shoves us in I think we should demand Home Rule for the marsh and declare UDI.' He squeezed in beside me and, under the cover of the chorus of approval and speculations on the precise placing of Customs posts along the Marsh Ditch, shot me his most charming smile and edged me out. His smile was as charming as his exceptionally good-looking face. He was of distant Anglo-Irish provenance, the third generation of his family born on the marsh, and he wore his dark curly hair and sideburns just long enough to appease his younger and not offend his older patients. He was

47

slightly shorter and considerably slighter than David, and a month younger than me. He lowered his voice to confide: 'I've only just got here and can't stay much longer. This is Father's half-day. I've still eight house calls before evening surgery. No peace for the wicked.' My expected response made him fondle my elbow. 'Dear little Rose,' he murmured. 'I wonder if you know how dear you are to me?'

I knew precisely, but didn't hold that against him. Having been poor, I knew rich was better and that he found me mildly sexually attractive and had convinced himself he was the right husband for me. If we had been born in our parents' generation he might have been right. We liked each other, had shared roots, similar tastes in music and books, and I would have accepted as the natural order the ex-public-schoolboy's patronising attitude to women he had not yet outgrown. But even without my genetic problem, nothing would persuade me to marry him, as much for his sake as mine. He would find marriage to me hell. I could keep up the little-woman act socially, when it suited me, but not permanently. I had come a long way from the naive teenage virgin Charles had married to appease current conventions. But in one respect I hadn't altered: I had always detested being fondled by a man I didn't love. I asked if he'd seen David. 'Seems to have vanished.'

He let go of my elbow. 'Just chatted to him out front with Duncan's lot. Looking very fit, I thought.'

I smiled my little-woman's smile. 'Very fit. Oh – found her, Harry?'

Harry shook his head dejectedly. 'Afternoon, Doctor. Hillman running nicely?'

'Like a bird since you serviced her, Harry. Sorry, must push off. *A bientôt*. Rose.'

I also had a French O Level. '*Au'voir*, Julian.'

Harry sighed. 'Time I scarpered, Mrs Endel. I told Chrissie just the hour. She's off till six but I got to get back. She wants to hang on she can get herself back.' He blushed. 'That make me a hog?'

I smiled normally and shook my head. 'We'll run her back. But she may be in the front garden.'

'She better! Ta, Mrs Endel.' He charged after Julian, disappearing round the side of the house. No other guests were showing any sign of leaving and the waitresses were offering little bowls of strawberries and cream. I looked around as if for a particular face, smiled into mid-air and made purposefully for a wrought-iron, white-painted seat that was down a side path at the end of the garden, hidden between great bushes of yellow, magenta and silvery-pink shrub roses.

'Aren't you clever to find somewhere to sit!' Sandra Black, looking even more a thirtyish Ophelia in floating grey nylon voile, her damp pale hair straggling round her narrow shoulders, sank down beside me. 'My feet are killing me but such a smashing party! Oh, God –' she giggled, 'I shouldn't have said that after a funeral. And you're "family".'

'Only very distantly, and it's the kind of send-off Lady Gillon would have wanted. She loved parties.'

'Thank God for that! I'm always saying the wrong thing. Makes Steve so mad.' She checked her flushed, ethereal face in her compact mirror and dabbed on powder. 'How in hell do you look so cool?'

'Lost the toss and driving.'

'Like Steve. Not that he ever lets me drive him. He says

women are lousy drivers.' She snapped shut her compact. 'He's in the front with the others but I needed a break. Chrissie's holding forth – just runs on and on –' she had drunk too much to conceal her jealousy – 'not that the men seem to mind.'

I chalked up one to David and looked at her with new interest. 'She's very attractive and sexy.'

'I suppose she is in an obvious sort of way. Personally, I think sexy people are far more attractive when it's less obvious. Take your chum David.' She waved at me with her empty glass. 'You have to look at him twice to spot he's sexy as hell. Brainy chaps often are in a frightening sort of way, though I don't suppose you've spotted that.'

I never argued with drunks. 'You could be right.'

She turned belligerent. 'I'm always right! Steve says that my one real contribution to our business is I can always spot a con or a fake. That's how I only had to see you and David together yesterday to spot you're not sleeping together. You don't really like men but even if you did, you and David just couldn't communicate.'

I was entranced. 'It's that obvious?'

'God, yes! You're far too artistic. Duncan says you draw rather well and have a real appreciation of music and David's got a razor-sharp mind, a double first in physics, a PhD and will probably collect a Nobel Prize before he's through. Being frightfully musical I know we artistic people just can't communicate with soulless scientists that work with things like computers. Different for Chrissie, of course – she's got quite a nice little soprano, but she's far too practical to be really artistic. I'm sure that's why she's a nurse. Nurses do have to be frightfully practical and insensitive or they couldn't do all the ghastly things they have to do for their patients. She and David are communicating splendidly.'

'How splendid for them both. No, thanks –' A waitress had found us and was offering more champagne.

'I will, please.' Sandra held up her glass before either of us noticed her husband had followed the waitress. 'I adore champers. I can swig it by the gallon.'

'When you get the chance, my sweet, which isn't often,' snarled Steven Black as the waitress vanished. His saturnine face had a greyish pallor and his eyes had narrowed to dark slits. 'That's your last for now. You may have forgotten we've a shop to run, I haven't.'

'Don't fuss, Steve! I must take this slowly. I'm a bit tight.'

'So what else is new?' He spat the words as David and Christine joined us and Sandra's flush purpled.

'Nowt for our Rose,' put in David. 'Known me years and still gives me house-room.'

I said, 'You said it, chum, not me.' And as he had defused the situation, Sandra laughed with the others.

Christine smiled at me with the deference due to a wife rather than a hostess. Having been a wife I registered the difference and raised her IQ. She looked vitally attractive in a mandarin-collared, short-sleeved black linen shift and exuded the confidence of a woman enjoying playing off one man against another. She said, 'I expect he's a perfect guest.'

'And always makes his own bed no matter how stoned when he drops into it.'

David said, 'May your milk of human charity never run dry, Rose, for you're going to need more. Duncan's Mini's packed it in again. Harry's gone so I've had a look. Wiring's gone beyond a patch-up job. All right with you if we give him a tow to George Ames's joint then run him home? He's got a rope in his boot.'

'Fine.' I stood up and looked at my watch. 'I told Harry we'd run you back, Christine. If we leave now we should easily make it by six.'

'Thanks awfully, Rose, if you're –'

'No need for that, Chrissie.' Steven cut her short. 'We're off now. We'll take you. But why's Harry ditched you?'

Christine's dimples deepened. 'You know Harry, Steve.'

His brows met. 'You mean you've had another set-to. God help you two when you marry.'

'Not "when", Steve. If.'

'None of my business either way. Time I got back to my own. Get moving, women!' He gave me an oddly formal little bow, nodded at David and strode off. Sandra followed, muttering apologetically.

Christine lingered and looked from David to me. 'I feel awful rushing off and not helping hitch up Duncan's car. I'm afraid he's working himself up into another state. But – well – Steve may need a bit of help with Sandra. She hasn't actually drunk too much, but it never takes much to get her sloshed. I think – I've thought for some time – she may have a mild diabetic problem. I've suggested she gets tested.' She shrugged. 'She won't hear of it. She's terrified of needles. Quite a lot of patients are. But I'd better dash. Do excuse me and thanks again for offering me a lift. Be seeing you.' She hurried after the others.

David watched them over the shrub roses that were higher than my head. 'What's Steve's provenance?'

'Londoner. South London from his and Sandra's

voices.' I thought of his bow. 'He could be the first English generation of Middle-European immigrants.'

'Yep. His bone structure and colouring are more Slav than Latin.' He turned to me. 'Mind my lumbering you with our Dunk?'

I smiled. 'No. Anyway, I owe him one.'

He nodded absently. 'Let's have your keys and I'll fix the tow while you say your piece to Maria. I've said mine and left Dunk metaphorically weeping on her shoulder. He's reacting as if he's just found a bomb under his bonnet.'

'He's always blown all fuses after minor mishaps, and as he's been off-balance since Max died, this afternoon'll have pushed him closer to the edge without any help from his wiring.'

'Figures.' He pocketed my keys. 'Let's git.'

We began walking quickly back through the garden, but were stopped by several friends wanting to fix up dates during his visit. It was nearly six when we left Littlehythe, and just after seven when we crossed the two-lane stone bridge over the Marsh Ditch at the inland foot of Cliffhill.

Duncan sat slumped on the back seat, his bushy hair a white halo, his pink, glistening, foxy face as distraught as when I picked him up on Thursday. I had shed my hat and both men their jackets; all the car windows were open and David was chain-smoking; but the smell of mothballs was near-throttling.

Duncan talked incessantly. 'One can only be humbled by the Gillons' courage and the warmth of their hospitality. And Henry most generously says we may continue to use his dear mother's music room on Thursdays for the time being until he and Maria have decided whether to sell the house or move down and put their own on the market. Only too understandably they are reluctant to abandon their exquisite garden, and such a blessed relief to know there will be no immediate disruption to our music-making – but how will one bear to set foot in Potts again without –' he broke off. 'No! One mustn't dwell! One must remember the living – our concert – oh my miserable wiring! David, are you convinced George Ames will have my Mini back Thursday morning?'

'Yes.'

I said, 'George is as reliable as Walt, Duncan. He won't let you down.'

'Bless you, my dear. Always the comforting word. What would I do without you? What would we all do without you?' He paused expectantly and as David stayed silent, returned to the Gillons. 'Such a gallant example of practical Christianity to us all. One must endure but not indulge grief and rejoice for those one has loved that they have gone to eternal peace . . .'

He talked on and on. I put in an occasional comment. David said nothing and I recognised from the abstracted quality of his silence that he was working on a mental problem. I wondered what had sparked this off, then had to shelve the matter. The heavy holiday traffic on the narrow, dyke-lined marsh roads demanded that I concentrate on driving. Even so, I became increasingly conscious of a vague and irrational sense of foreboding that I couldn't dispel.

Duncan only stopped talking when I turned into the side road that was a short-cut to St Martin's. This road ran into Sea Lane, which twisted round the outskirts of the village and at one point ran straight for a couple of hundred yards between corkscrew turns. Duncan's cottage was the only building on the left of the straight stretch and about a hundred yards down on the right were the two semi-detached cottages the Dawsons had made into one. From their closed windows and garage doors, they were not yet home. The lane around was empty and Duncan's front gate hung open.

'That wretched boy Tommy Burt has a head like a sieve!' He teetered. 'I disremember the times I've told him to leave the evening paper on the front step and close the gate.'

David surfaced. 'Looks as if he's chucked it in through your front door and forgotten to close that.' He spoke before I could kick him silent. I had noticed the door was ajar and, knowing Duncan's obsession for locking up even if only strolling along to talk to the Dawsons over their front gate, had been about to break this more gently.

'Oh, no, no! It shouldn't be open!' His voice rose hysterically. 'I know I locked it! Only I have the key – see! It must be – oh no –' he was gasping like an asthmatic. 'No, not burglars! Not after so much –' he grasped my shoulders. 'I can't take any more.'

'You may have forgotten to lock it –'

'We all have our off moments.'

David and I spoke together. He added, 'I'll take a look.' He was out of the car and half-way up the front path before I shook off Duncan's hands and unclipped my safety-belt.

I swung open my door. 'Hang about, David –' but he had pushed open the front door and gone inside. The door suddenly slammed shut and almost simultaneously I heard a heavy thud. I leapt out of the car, raced up the path, tried the doorknob and as it was unlocked, kicked the door wide open. On the doorstep I stopped, momentarily transfixed with horror. The door opened into Duncan's sitting room that now looked as if it had been hit by a hurricane. David was sprawled face down amongst the debris, blood streaming from a large gash behind his left ear, and his unbroken glasses on the floor a few feet from his head.

I was suddenly too angry for horror. I dived for David, yelling, 'Duncan, come quick!' I slid a hand under David's face and felt his breath on my palm and heard Duncan panting up the path.

He gasped from the doorway, 'No! No! Is he – ?'

'No! Unconscious. See if that phone's working and –'

'I – no – not yet – must sit – I'll have a stroke –'

'You can't have one!' I hauled a clean handkerchief from one of David's trouser pockets, flipped it into a pad and pressed it hard on the gash. 'I've got to stop this bleeding. Try the phone. If it's working don't waste time ringing 999 as that goes through to Astead and it'll be ages before help reaches us. Ring Julian Carmody at the St Martin's surgery first, then PC Parker, then Walt Ames. Tell 'em I said so.'

'Surely Parker first – he – he – could still be hiding upstairs and –'

'If he is I'll bloody kill him!' With my free hand I turned David's face to one side and loosened his tie. 'Stop messing about, man! If that phone works ring Julian *now*! If it's bust get into my car and get him!'

David gave a long sigh and without opening his eyes said dazedly, but clearly, 'For Christ's sake, Duncan, do as she says unless you want to risk facing a charge of accessory to murder. If Rose lays a hand on the sod

56

manslaughter won't stick. She's an Endel.' He gave another sigh and passed out again. And as again I felt his breath on my palm I heard a motorbike going placidly down the lane towards the sea.

FOUR

DAVID TOOK OFF HIS GLASSES TO STUDY HIS REFLEC-tion in the shaving-mirror I had just handed him. The blotches under his bloodshot eyes were purple, the grazed lump over his left temple was blackish-red, his tan was yellowish and a thickly padded adhesive dressing slanted from the back of his left ear to the nape of his neck. 'Best pair of shiners I've had in years.'

'Julian said inevitable after a bad clout on the back of the head.' (And that had he been hit another inch to the right it would probably have killed him.) I poured his morning tea and sat on the side of his bed. 'How do you feel?'

'I've had worse hangovers.' He re-angled the mirror to expose his dressing. 'That shot he gave me before putting in the stitches had me out so fast I can only remember the first. How many?'

'Fourteen.' I spoke calmly, to cover my anxiety and still seething anger. 'He said your memory would prob-ably be dodgy for a day or so and perhaps longer, or might suddenly clear, and he couldn't be more specific as concussion affects individuals in individual ways. He'll be here after morning surgery and said as the shot would have worn off and the sedatives you had later weren't painkillers and you would almost certainly wake with a crashing headache, you could have a couple of paracetamol.' I produced a bottle from my jeans pocket. 'Take them with your tea?'

'Not right now, thanks.' He replaced his glasses, put the mirror on his bedside table and leant stiffly back against the pillows I had just piled behind him and used in his armchair during the night. 'My mind's doped enough.' He picked up his tea and drank thirstily. 'I'll get up in a few minutes.'

'Over my dead body. If I hadn't promised Julian I'd keep you in bed you'd now be in Cliffhill General.'

He smiled. 'Balls, love. Our Jule's not as thick as he looks. He knew bloody well that if he overruled my refusal to be hospitalised while he had me under, soon as I surfaced I'd discharge myself. One of the few times I can remember is his saying he couldn't feel a skull fracture.'

'Or rule out a hairline crack without an X-ray.'

'Oh, aye.' He drank more tea. 'One of my mates in the States is a cranial surgeon and like all medics never stops talking shop. He says no better treatment for a hairline than rest and quiet. I'll get far more of both here than in any hospital bed.'

'Julian said something like that before he left.' I didn't add that this had been after he and Walt had helped David on to his bed, put on his pyjamas and seen his scars. Julian, his face professionally bland, then added, 'One can appreciate that he's had enough of hospitals,' and Walt nodded woodenly.

59

Last night the news had been all round St Martin's long before closing time. Early this morning Murdo, morose and monosyllabic, had removed Jody and an hour ago Marlene and Daph arrived on their mopeds looking as if they had come to pay their last respects. Marlene was now pussy-footing round the flat with a dustpan and broom to avoid the noise of the vacuum cleaner.

'Parker been up, Rosie?' David asked.

I shook my head. 'Julian told him no visitors, including cops, until he sees you again.'

'Remind me to buy him a drink.' He frowned in thought. 'Christ, is my bloody mind AWOL. I've only a vague recollection of making a statement to Parker. Pre-shot?' I nodded. 'What did I tell him?'

I only hesitated briefly. Julian had insisted that this morning I must try and keep David's mind off what PC Parker termed 'the incident'. Julian was a good GP and having risen to junior surgical registrar in his qualifying hospital, St Benedict's, London, before he decided to join his father's practice, had been a particular godsend last night, but he didn't know David well enough to realise that once conscious, with or without a crashing head-ache, only the truth would appease him. 'That you neither saw nor heard who clouted you, but thought something must have struck you as wrong when you pushed open the door, as you did remember taking off your glasses. We'd found them on the floor and thought they'd been jerked off your face by the force of the blow.'

'Can't remember if I chucked 'em clear. What did he use? Any leads?'

I looked at him blankly. 'A brass poker's missing.'

He reached for one of my hands. 'Cool it, Rosie. Dead-loss Lofthouse I may be, but I ain't dead yet. What else is missing?'

'I don't know. When we left Duncan was still incoherent with shock and Parker and the two CID men from Astead were busy with their tape measures.'

He blinked painfully. 'How did the plainclothes get in on the act?'

'Parker's duty-sergeant whistled them up after Parker rang him from Duncan's. They were on the marsh investigating a series of caravan break-ins at Lynstreet. Only eight miles from St Martin's so they horsed over. They think the same gang might be involved.'

He nodded and patently wished he hadn't. 'Why wasn't the phone cut off?'

'Parker said because this mob aren't real pros and just tearaways down on day trips from London for anything they can pick up. According to him no real pro would have left the phone in good order or made such a dog's dinner of the cottage and the lock on the kitchen window. The front door lock wasn't forced – Duncan must've forgotten to lock it. Parker thinks the chap only discovered it was unlocked once he got in through the kitchen window and was about to leave by the front when we arrived, so he backed behind the door in panic, let you have it and nipped out via the kitchen. Good cover that way. The back garden has a high hedge and there's a grazing field between it and the back gardens of the nearest cottages. My guess is that once Duncan came inside, the man nipped round to the front and up or down the lane. I heard a motorbike going by, but too slowly for anyone in a hurry. Most of the village men have them. It could have been one going home for tea. If it was, Parker'll have his name by now. If he's a stranger, someone will have seen him. Sea Lane looked empty when we stopped, but there's always a shepherd or hedger-and-ditcher or bird-watcher or someone walking a dog somewhere around. Someone in the country always sees everything.'

'A city lad won't know that. I only caught on in End.' He lit a cigarette, took a couple of puffs and stubbed it out. 'Wish to hell I could remember what struck me as wrong.'

That barely smoked cigarette told me how he felt. 'Don't fight it, David. Give the rest and quiet a try.'

'No bloody alternative till Jule's sedatives wear off. What were they?' I told him and he grimaced. 'Bloody knockouts. No wonder I can't even remember how old Walt came into the act.'

Thank God for that. He had been hurt enough. 'I sent for him. He lives near and I wanted someone I trusted to handle Duncan while I dealt with you. You were bleeding like a stuck pig and Duncan was so hysterical he was quite likely to start tidying up before Parker arrived. Walt came first, then Julian, then Parker, as he'd just got home to Shepland for tea.' Shepland was a large village ten miles from St Martin's and both were in PC Parker's patch. 'The DS and DC showed up about thirty minutes later.' There was a soft tap on the door. 'Just see what Marlene wants.'

'Let's have her in.'

I looked at him quickly. He had little personal vanity, but he wasn't an exhibitionist. 'Julian won't approve.' He raised two fingers. I smiled and opened the door.

'Morning, Marlene! How goes it?'

'Oh, Mr Lofthouse!' Marlene clapped her hands to her

face. 'Your poor face – your poor head! What he done to you?'

'Nothing to what I'd like to do to him. Want me out of bed so you can do this room?'

She glanced at me, read the message in my eyes and came in, raising a finger at David. 'Don't you think of stirring, Mr Lofthouse! You stay where you are and I'll give the lick and the promise round – oh, Miss Rose, I'm forgetting. Mr Ames is waiting in the office.'

'Thanks, Marlene.' I closed the door on them and leant against it. It had been a long night and neither Jody nor I had had much sleep. She had spent it on the floor beside David's armchair and every time I reached out and touched him to reassure myself he was alive, she raised her head to watch me. I had spent hours chasing mental shadows that in the pre-dawn silence, when even the frogs slept, had begun to coalesce into a nebulous pattern with as many blank patches as David's present memory. That he wanted to talk privately to Marlene illuminated one of those patches. Walt could be about to illuminate another. He never wasted time or words. He hadn't left the farm on a working morning at the height of the hay-baling and sheep-sheering season to pay a social call.

I went quickly along my flat's L-shaped corridor to the short arm off which, on the outer side, lay my office and dining room that had been made by dividing the former morning room. 'Good morning, Walt. Sorry to keep you waiting.'

Walt, short and thickset, stood by the flat-topped desk dangling from one hand the old brown trilby he wore in summer. His boots were newly rinsed, brown cords embedded with hayseeds, and his blue cotton, short-sleeved shirt was impeccably starched and ironed. Mrs

Walt had worked in a Cliffhill hand-laundry before she married; Walt and Kevin's shirts were her pride, and the sorrow of her elder son's teenage wife.

'Morning, madam. I just stopped by with the farm post and not fetched it down with one of the lads as I want a look at Glebe field before shifting down a flock this afternoon.' He handed me a stack of mail that by long prearrangement he had opened. 'Just wait while you check.'

'Thanks.' I sat at the desk. 'Do sit.'

'All right as I am, ta, madam.'

I glanced through the post. 'No problems here.'

'Nah.' He didn't move and his brick-red face and deep-set blue eyes were calm as the sea this morning. 'Best. You'll have more than the farm on your mind. How's Mr Lofthouse keeping?'

'Only just woken and looking as if he's gone a few rounds with Mohammed Ali. He says he's had worse hangovers. I wouldn't bet on it.' I sat back in my swivel chair. 'I don't like having a guest beaten up on our home territory, Walt.'

'Not right, madam.' There was a rare undercurrent of anger in his slow, broad-vowelled voice. 'Mind you . . .' he smoothed his thinning fair hair, 'for all the young doctor says of his luck being in not copping it more to the right, I shouldn't wonder if Mr Morgan had the better luck. If he'd come back on his tod and walked into what was waiting, not have done a chap his age much good and no saying when he'd have been found, seeing the door slammed shut. Open again when young Kevin went by, and seeing your car he just reckoned you was paying a call.'

64

I sat straighter. 'That was Kevin's motorbike?'

'Seemly, madam. Just coming home for his tea and taking the short-cut same as always and taking it easy like as he should, having picked up the two cautions for speeding. He got home just after I left and seeing I just told my wife you wanted me, she told him I gone down to Endel. He finished his tea, got back on his bike, picked up young Linda Burt up Shepland and took her to the pictures up Cliffhill. Time he got back my wife and I gone to bed. Kevin didn't know where to put his face when I told him this morning what he missed. I had him give Sam Parker the tinkle before he left for work and he said to tell you he's ever so sorry he didn't think to stop when you was needing a hand.'

'Not his fault. Did he see anyone else around Sea Lane?'

He nodded calmly. 'Old Biffer Irons running his dog back of Major Dawson's. Old Biffer gave him a wave, he told Sam, so Sam got on his bike for a word with Biffer. But from what Sam told me when he stopped by the farm an hour back, Biffer didn't see more than Kevin.' He rubbed his formidable and invariably clean-shaven jaw reflectively. 'Not best pleased this morning, is Sam Parker. He knows that poker's down a dyke and if Mr Morgan's bits of silver gone up London he'll not see 'em back.'

I looked at him for a few moments. He thought far more quickly than he spoke and he never spoke without forethought. Having to leave school and start full-time work at thirteen had limited his vocabulary, but not his intelligence. He was a top-class farm manager and I had learned to trust absolutely in his farming expertise, knowledge of the marsh, weather forecasts and judgement of men. And also to understand his unspoken language. 'Silver worth much?'

'I'd not say so for all Mr Morgan's carrying on like he's lost the Crown Jewels. Just the small teapot, milk jug, sugar basin he had from his old mum but not proper old, just Edwardian and more like silver plate than silver from the description he give Sam. Sam reckons a real pro not have touched it but might have looked worth a few quid to a lad not knowing better. Mind you, madam, he'll know what it cost if they get him. First offence or not, he'll do time for breaking and entry, burglary and GBH.'

I mentally noted that 'if'. 'Doesn't sound worth doing time for.'

He said without a flicker of emotion, 'Not if he just nicked it to flog it.'

My mind shot back to my thoughts in the night. 'You think he only took it to make it look like a burglary?' His slight nod tingled the back of my neck. 'Waiting for Mr Morgan and got the wrong man?'

'Mr Morgan's cottage, madam.'

'Yes. Who's got it in for him, Walt?'

'I can't put a name to the one. Sam neither. One of the London mob, he says, back up London last night and that's the last we'll hear of him. The Met's got enough on their plate without wasting police time on a small job down here that's left Mr Lofthouse with no worse than a sore bonce. Mind you –' he paused deliberately – 'as I told Sam the hour back, if Mr Lofthouse been a goner he'd have had more than the two Astead lads on his patch last night and I shouldn't wonder if today the Chief Constable had fetched down half the top brass from

County HQ and a couple of lads from the Yard. If you'll pardon the liberty, madam, wouldn't Mr Lofthouse be one of the nobs in his business?'

My mouth had dried. 'He's never said so but that's my impression.'

'No surprise to me, madam. Thirteen pence in the shilling is Mr Lofthouse, I told Sam and he didn't argue. He's wanting another word with him as soon as Young Doctor says, and with you.'

'Any time, far as I'm concerned.'

'I'll tell him. I'll be off down Glebe. You'll tell Mr Lofthouse I was asking for him?'

'Of course. Thanks for coming.'

'I had to come by, madam.' He went out, slapping on his hat and closing the door behind him.

Yes, I thought, he had to. He doesn't like the smell of this, either. I swung my chair round to face the open window. I watched his elderly Land Rover go down the drive and take the left turn just beyond End Cottage which ran on past the Glebe field that one of my Tudor ancestors had bought – or grabbed – when Henry VIII was dissolving monasteries and selling church land.

Being on one of the lowest parts of Midstreet the field was only suitable for sheep after a longish, hot, dry spell. This morning was hot enough for August and the lazily incoming tide so far out that patches of silvery sand glittered in the sunshine. The coastguard's red flag was up to warn of quicksand. I had never known that warning to be necessary. No locals swam off Midstreet and few visitors even bothered to climb the sea wall to look down at a beach swamped by every high tide, when a few miles north and south were miles of safe beaches with car and caravan parks. I looked for some time at the red flag hanging limply from a metal pole embedded in the concrete top of the wall. A wooden pole would be snapped like a matchstick by its first encounter with a south-east gale. Strong stuff metal, I thought and shuddered. Then a flash of sunlight on a dark green Hillman turning off the coast road jerked me to my feet. I went back to David. Marlene had finished his room and made him fresh tea and toast. The toast was untouched and his cleaned ashtray empty.

'Julian in sight and Walt said to tell you he was asking for you. How's the hangover?'

'Shifting, thanks. What's Walt just said that's bugging you?'

I stuck to the facts and told him about Duncan's silver briefly, and not only because the car was nearing the house. 'What's bugging me is your getting clobbered.'

'My own bloody fault for sticking my neck out. But I'm hellishly sorry to have lumbered you with the aftermath.'

'Forgotten I dropped you into it?'

'Like hell you did.' He looked at me over his glasses. 'You didn't ask me to spend this vacation in Endel, bump off Lady G., bugger up Dunk's wiring, or ask me to nip out and pick up his evening paper. By what right do you deny my own right to take chances?'

I stared at him as if he had spoken in a foreign language. 'Had his wiring been buggered up?' I spoke fast; Julian's car was crawling round to the back. 'That what was bugging you on the drive back? Or can't you remember?'

He hesitated, then said, 'Dimly. Didn't he give us a running commentary?' I nodded as my front doorbell rang and Marlene scampered to answer it. 'Later, love. Let's have him in.'

I opened the door. 'Morning, Julian, he's all yours.'

'Good morning to you both.' Julian came in briskly, smiling professionally and oozing aftershave, carbolic soap and reassurance. 'You're leaving us, Rose?'

'What else? After the times I've heard you and your father beefing about relatives and friends cluttering up bedsides when you want privacy with your patients.'

'What can I say to that, David?'

'You're the doc, mate.'

I said, 'How about, "A word with you later, Rose."?'

'My pleasure.' Julian ushered me out and the still hovering Marlene all but strong-armed me into the kitchen. This had been the former butler's pantry and had a side door into the front hall.

'It's not right, Miss Rose!' Marlene's pleasant face blazed with anger. 'It's not right what he done to poor Mr Lofthouse as never done harm to none and is a real nice gentleman for all he comes from up Yorkshire – can't help that, can he? Cruel poorly, he is – just the one fag-end good as new – just shows, that does. I dunno what's happening to folks these days. Never used to have nothing like this down the marsh when I was a kiddie. Never had to lock a door.'

I glanced at the side door. 'We've always had a few home-grown thugs, Marlene.'

'I'm not saying we not had the few,' she retorted, 'and still got 'em – but not real nasty like this lot down from London. They're all saying up the village it was one of them that done Mr Lofthouse for barging in whiles he was helping hisself to Mr Morgan's old mum's silver teapot and the like. And what I says is, it's a mercy the

69

kiddies as should've been here got the mumps. Mr Lofthouse just been telling me how you had to open up the front door for the Young Doctor and Mr Ames to fetch him out the doctor's car and bring him in through, the hall being easier. Not right for little kiddies to see, that wasn't. Sensitive they are, the poor little loves, and would be, wouldn't they? Could have spoiled their holidays shocking and given them nightmares ever so long.'

I looked at her for a few moments. 'Yes. Lucky they had to cancel.' My telephone was ringing. 'I'll get it. Please bring the doctor along if he's done before I've rung off.' I shot on to the office, leaving its door and my mental filing cabinet open. I always did a re-check before filing anything literally, or mentally.

'Darling! Henry's just rung from his office about poor David!' Maria's voice nearly pierced my eardrum. 'What actually happened? . . . Oh, God! . . . Oh, no! Julian with him now? . . . You must be absolutely shattered! . . . Oh, poor house-proud Duncan . . . I'll ring him after this . . . Thanks, darling, yes, everyone says it went off rather well – poor darling Mama would have been so touched . . . Oh, yes, still shattered, poor sweetie! But getting back to the office will help, as he does so love his sums . . . Yes, I'm sure you're hectic, but hang on a tick, Rose. I need you to help me with Mama's clothes. Henry says I must deal with them and I can't face it with just Nora. She'll be in floods and so will I. I was going to suggest tomorrow, but if that's too soon for you how about Friday, fourish? I've a Cliffhill Floral Soc. meeting in the morning and a PCC at 2.30 but that seldom lasts more than an hour . . . You will if David's OK? Darling, you're

70

a sweetie! Julian leaving? . . . Love to David and I'll ring tomorrow – cheers!'

I replaced the receiver. 'Time for a coffee, Julian?'

'Alas, no, but thanks for the kind thought.' He put his medical bag on my desk and glanced round the office that I kept closed when entertaining socially. 'First time I've been in here. Very businesslike. I'm impressed.'

Gratitude insisted I let that pass. 'How is he?'

'Picking up nicely, but I've told him to stay where he is until I see him tomorrow.' He glanced over his shoulder. 'May I close that door for a moment?' He didn't wait for my response. 'Strictly between ourselves, as I don't want him running before he can walk, though he's still having the mental confusion that's a typical post-concussive symptom, he is in better shape than I would have expected had I not seen his multiple scars. To have made such an excellent recovery he must have tremendous physical and mental resilience and stamina. Both are invaluable medical allies and his being a strong, healthy chap of thirty-six adds to that score. Nevertheless –' he smiled conspiratorially – 'I did suggest he improve his general health by stopping smoking.'

'How did he take it?'

'Very sensibly. He's going to work on it.'

My eyes widened. 'Nice one, Julian. I've never made first base on that.'

'Dear little Rose.' His tone patted me on the head. 'Only too obvious why he needs the crutch when you are around and he has spent the past few years working abroad. I have to admit –' he paused as if to choose his words – 'that for some time your relationship with David has puzzled and – er – perturbed me. I now realise with shame that I have misjudged you both. Can you forgive me?'

My gratitude had its limits. When treated as a child, I could act the child. 'For what?'

'For not realising until last night that all you feel for him is the great affection of an old friend. Only too understandably that's not enough for David, so being a decent chap, he's largely removed himself from your life. But had you been seriously emotionally involved with him you couldn't possibly have maintained the admirable detachment with which you dealt with his injuries and the general situation last night. Where did you learn first aid?'

'Nowhere specific. Just picked up bits from farm accidents. Isn't it mostly common sense?'

'To a certain extent. But the shock of finding him unconscious and oozing gore would have had most girls hysterical. Your self-control astounds me. I should add that when I passed this on to my father he reminded me that you were an Endel and that the Endels were renowned for keeping their heads in tight corners.'

I said drily, 'Well, thanks – and nothing to forgive.'

There was a small flare of triumph in his eyes. 'Thank you. I must push off.' He took a longer look at the row of filing cabinets and the heavy, metal safe bolted to one inner wall as if deciding the office would do very nicely for his secretary. 'If you'll forgive the gratuitous medical advice, take things easy today. Leave the farm business in Walt's capable hands, or better still, hire a secretary. You are looking far too tired and carrying too much on your small shoulders.'

I stifled the urge to remind him that unlike most women of my age I had no responsibilities to a husband

and children, or domestic or financial problems, and that most people looked tired after a bad night. I thanked him for the advice and all his help.

'Only too thankful to be there when you needed me, Rose. Any time – just pick up a phone. You take it easy. I'll see myself out. I know the way.' He backed out, closing the door, and I heard him talking to Marlene and then the click of her shutting the front door.

I didn't watch him drive away. I sat on my desk and got down to some mental filing. I was still at it when David knocked and called quietly, 'May I intrude briefly?'

'Sure.' I opened the door. 'Why aren't you in bed?'

'Just had a shower and needing exercise.' He had shaved and combed his hair, put on clean blue cotton pyjamas and his navy-silk dressing-gown and the bruises on his taut, yellowish face stood out even more sharply than in bed. 'Julian said bath not to wet the dressing so I borrowed your shower cap.'

'Won't have struck him I possessed one. Sit down, man.' I pushed him into my chair and sat facing him on the edge of the desk.

'Nice to meet a lad that's led a blameless life. Not that many left now they hand out the pill on the NHS. He's younger than me but we were both born too soon to cash in on that. Our life on the campus was so bloody segregated that it was an erotic thrill to sit next to a woman in a lecture room. What did he say about me?'

'That you're doing nicely, must take things quietly, being very sensible and going to cut smoking.'

He smiled, 'Hell, love, if we're not put into this world to lighten the paths of others, why are we here? As I hadn't then taken a look at his handiwork in the triple-

73

mirror in your spare bathroom, I didn't remind him smoking's not the only way of shortening one's life.' His smile vanished and we exchanged a long look. 'Yes,' he said as if I had spoken, 'another inch right and you'd now be ringing old Smith to alter your bloody will.'

I had to swallow to speak. 'Not my Mr Smith. He died this January and his nephew Edward's now senior partner.'

'Any good?'

'Younger, so more human, but otherwise chip off the old block.'

His face hardened. 'Which means he objects strongly to your choice of heir-apparent.'

This was another old battle that I had won and would win again. I didn't want to re-fight it now. 'Naturally. Smith, Smith and Smith have been the Endels' solicitors since his great-grandfather founded the firm. Of course he wants the status quo and the entail to continue indefinitely.'

'Does he know you've told me I'm in line for the loot I don't bloody want?' I nodded reluctantly. 'Christ, woman! Had you nipped out to pick up that paper, odds-on I'd now be helping Sam and his mates with their inquiries. High time you thought of my health and altered that bloody will!'

I shook my head. 'Sorry. Thinking of my health – and when I gave Edward only half of my reasons for why you, he said he could not, hand on heart, advise me to do otherwise.'

David's rising temper was visibly worsening his head-ache. 'Unless he only said that to keep in good with you, you need another solicitor. You are prejudiced in my favour and he's never met me. He can't know I'm not a devious sod on the make.'

I had to stop this with a knockout. 'He doesn't have to take my word for it that you're not. He's not just my Mr Smith's nephew. General Wenden married his father's twin sister and Sir Norman Hurst's his godfather. And in case you've blanks on this – he's still Chief Constable and the president of your marsh fan club. General Wenden's the vice-p. and Walt the hon. sec.' He raised his hands in surrender but I hadn't finished. 'Yes, Endel's worth collecting, but it's not worth the risk of a life stretch to BCC's Einstein, Junior, who last time round in my presence the Chief Constable thanked for being the very useful unofficial eyes and ears of the county constabulary.' I heard what I had said, but as he had pulled off his glasses and slapped a hand over his eyes, he missed my reaction. 'BCC still paying you peanuts, duckie?'

He laughed. 'I need another shower.' He stood up, drew me off the desk and kissed me. 'Mmmm. You smell delicious. What is it?'

'That Chanel you sent me last Christmas. I got another bottle when I finished yours.'

'I'm glad you liked it. Suits you.' He kissed me again then suddenly his whole body tensed and he buried his face in my neck. 'Yes – that's it.' He straightened and took another deep breath. 'You minus mothballs.'

My mind did a double-take. 'It was something you smelt that made you take off your glasses.'

'Yes.' He put them on. 'Dunk's suit doused your scent in the car but I smelt it when I pushed open the door. I'm now remembering registering you were still in the car and Dunk unlikely to use it as an air-freshener or harbour a mistress with expensive tastes, just before I saw stars and blacked out. Anyone smelling it later would assume you brought it in.'

'David – so it could be a woman.'

'Unless the scent was sprayed to give that impression.'

'Yes,' I said, 'yes. Like nicking the silver.' I now told him all Walt had said about this. 'Walt doesn't like the smell and nor do I. Specifically now. If she's a woman, far too much of a coincidence that we use the same scent.'

'Coincidences do happen, Rosie. Hold it – curtain's lifting higher – he must have heard and probably seen your car stopping. A bloke in a blind panic would've beat it fast out back. Had enough time. Why wait behind the door?'

My mental pattern had reformed with a new and terrifying clarity. My headache until his clears, I thought. I said carefully, 'If he's an outsider he most probably wouldn't have recognised it wasn't Duncan's car, and was waiting to get him. As Walt said, Duncan's cottage and – hell!' My telephone was ringing. 'I'll say I must call back.' I grabbed the receiver. 'Midstreet 17 –'

'Good morning, Mrs Endel,' interrupted a headmistressy contralto, 'Miss Peters, Mr Edward Smith's secretary speaking. Mr Edward would very much appreciate a few moments of your time. May I put him through?'

David moved to the door. I beckoned him back. 'Please, Miss Peters.'

'Through now, Rose,' announced Edward's clipped voice. 'Good morning to you. I just want a brief word with you on a couple of matters. First, I'm extremely sorry to hear of the disgraceful attack on Dr Lofthouse last evening. How is he?'

I looked at David. 'Bit battered. How did you hear?'

'One of our typists is married to the Detective Sergeant

76

Brand dealing with these break-ins at Lynstreet. A very nasty incident, from her account. Far too many young thugs around these days. I have not yet had the pleasure of meeting Dr Lofthouse,' he went on with a pomposity that told me Miss Peters was listening, 'but pray convey to him my sympathies and best wishes for a speedy recovery.'

David bowed. I said, 'Thanks, Edward, I will. What's the second matter?'

'One upon which I shall be writing to you today. However, in view of last evening's unpleasantness, I thought a short verbal report of some rather surprising but not – I surmise – unpleasant news, might not come amiss.'

'You couldn't be more right. Let's have it.'

'Very well.' He sounded pleased. 'I have just received in this morning's post a communication from our colleagues John Watson and Partners of Cliffhill in connection with the last will and testament of their late client, Miss Eugenia Victoria Mercer, deceased, of Ferry Cottage, Littlemarsh Lane, Littlehythe in the county of Kent. Briefly, Rose, she has bequeathed to you Ferry Cottage, her small garden and garden produce, but not the contents of her cottage and other personal possessions.' He heard my sharp intake of breath. 'Indeed. Rather surprising.'

'Dumbfounding! Edward – why?'

'John Watson has not seen fit to enlighten me on that matter. Do you wish me to make discreet enquiries?'

I avoided looking at David and felt him watching me. 'Please.'

'I'll put it in hand. We must discuss this more fully, but as I've a client waiting, full day ahead and am due in

77

court all tomorrow, I have no free space until 11 a.m. on Friday. Could you come into Astead then?'

Being pay-day, Friday was my heaviest working day and I had already agreed to interrupt it for Maria. My common sense insisted I could perfectly well leave this until after David had gone. My common sense always lost out to my instincts. I said that would suit me fine. He said he would look forward to seeing me and we rang off.

'How much did you hear, David?'

'Enough to suggest you nip up to the second landing and apologise to Grandad's portrait for slapping on the paternity suit.'

I smiled wryly. 'I should've known you'd caught on.'

'Knowing you, how could I bloody not?' He now sounded exhausted. 'If the third war kicks off this afternoon you'll blame an Endel for pushing the button. Maybe it's my fault that you're stuck back in the old groove. When I left for the States you'd stopped thinking with your emotions and started using your bloody good brain. This time –' he shrugged – 'back to square one. Maybe it's the return of the wandering lad that's prised open the bloody Pandora's box and if so the best thing I can do for us both is to get out and stay out.' He glanced at the window. 'Shove that one on the back burner. Here's Sam Parker through the gates. I'll get back to bed. Jule said up to me if I saw him. Send him in when you want.'

I nodded tensely. 'Going to tell him you smelt that Chanel?'

'Not yet, if ever. I can't prove it. If this comes to court it'll be laughed out after Jule's medical evidence on my mental state last night and this morning.'

'If – not when?'

78

He blinked at me stolidly, 'Not if I smelt right. But I could be hallucinating. Want this door open or shut?'

'Open, please.'

He walked away as slowly as an old man and didn't see Marlene popping out of the kitchen and shaking her head at his back. I returned to the office window. The front door of the house was open and Sam Parker was slowing his motorbike by the mounting-block. Before he had swung off his machine and hitched it back on its stand, my confused mind had polarised on a single decision: until David left Endel, either Jody or I, and preferably both, must shadow him.

FIVE

'HASN'T HE EVEN TOLD YOU WHO GETS HER FURNI-
ture and things, Edward?'

'I'm afraid not, Rose.' Edward Smith sat back in his
mahogany, claw-armed chair and pressed his fingertips
together. He was a slight, neat, black-haired man in his
late forties with shrewd eyes and a long-jawed, uncom-
promisingly tough face. 'Very properly John Watson
never divulges more of a client's affairs than is essential
for an interested third party to know. However, as he
informed me over the phone earlier this morning that the
contents of Ferry Cottage are due to be cleared later
today, and as Charlotte tells me little in the vicinity of
Littlehythe escapes Maria Gillon, I think it not improbable that Maria may be able to provide some enlighten-
ment in this context at tomorrow's concert.'

'Possibly sooner.' I explained my date this afternoon. 'I
hope so. This isn't just idle curiosity. I want to know
since if it's another casual acquaintance it'll make more
sense of my legacy.'

'Why should it not make sense to you that a singularly – one could add, sadly – solitary old woman should choose to dispose of her property amongst her friends? In my experience that is a far from exceptional occurrence.'

'Because we weren't friends. She just chatted to me occasionally because she had liked my father.' His eyes flickered. 'You think that comes into it?'

He had little physical resemblance to his late uncle, but he shared his aversion to giving a straight answer to a straight question. 'That may or may not have been a contributory factor. Is that fan bothering you?'

'Slightly,' I lied, to gain thinking time.

He got up to adjust the portable electric fan he had switched on after closing the high sashed window to shut out the noise and fumes of the traffic in Astead high street. Astead was a large market-cum-light-industrial town thirteen miles inland from Coxden, on one of the main routes from London to the marsh coast, and the temperature in the town centre was now in the mid-eighties Fahrenheit. The heat had given me a cast-iron excuse for leaving Jody with David and asking him to keep her on the lead and in any shade going, if he felt like taking her for a stroll. He had accepted this with the new, uncharacteristic passivity that was rejoicing Julian '. . . trust a sensible chap to be sensible . . . ' but no others. It had plunged Marlene, Daph and Murdo into deepening gloom, and when Walt called after breakfast to collect the weekly wages cheque and cash it at the bank and heard David was not yet up, his face could have been carved out of igneous rock. 'He's not hisself yet, madam.'

'I'm afraid not. Parker come up with anything new?'

'Not so much as the one whisper, for all he's not got

cloth ears.' We exchanged a long, guarded look. 'Early days, mind.'

'Yes.' I recognised the brick wall and changed the subject. 'I'm seeing Mr Edward Smith about an estate matter at eleven. Astead'll be too hot for Jody so I'll leave her with Mr Lofthouse.'

'She'll be best out the sun. Right, then. 'Morning, madam.'

When I went into David's room to say I was off he was lying back against his pillows wearing dark glasses over his own, his curtains were half-drawn and ashtray empty. 'Take it easy till I'm back, David.'

'Trust me. Just a born layabout. You should try it, some time.'

Not right now, I thought, watching Edward deal with the fan. It was his only visible innovation since moving into the senior partner's traditional ground-floor front office in the Georgian house in the high street that had been his great-grandfather's matrimonial home, and was now wholly occupied by the firm. The office was decorated in drab browns and greens and even though the heavy Edwardian furniture and glass-fronted book-shelves lining the walls shone with polish, the general impression was of a comfortingly musty, old-fashioned stability.

'Better, Rose?'

'Fine, thanks.' I waited for him to sit down before I kicked him under the belt. 'Did Ginny Mercer once have an illegitimate baby, Edward?'

He slightly raised one black eyebrow. 'My dear girl, surely you give no credence to old wives' tales?'

'Not in general. This one interests me mainly because I only heard it by chance since her death. But as you were born and lived in St Martin's till you married, presumably you heard it ages ago. Right?' He nodded slightly. 'When?'

'Who can date the folklore of one's childhood? That slander was ancient history before I was packed off to prep school. However, I can tell you I've never known of one shred of evidence to support it. Now the poor woman's dead, why dig it up?'

'Because when I started wondering why it took so long to reach me and belatedly discovered she had worked in Endel as a girl, it struck me that probably my grandfather made her pregnant.'

He was a good lawyer. He didn't even blink. 'On what grounds do you base that slanderous assumption?'

He wasn't my lover, I was paying for his time and to use it I had worked three hours in my office before breakfast. 'Hunch.'

'Which I would have assumed this legacy should now demolish.'

I thought of David's reaction. My judgement agreed with both men; not my instincts. But as there was a limit to the number of men I wanted to convince I needed psychiatric therapy, I nodded. 'Had my hunch been on the ball I wouldn't have expected her to leave a brass farthing to an Endel.' I thought of Ginny Mercer's old, unyielding face and shook my head instinctively. 'I just wish I knew why she chose me. She didn't owe me any favours – and please don't tell me not to look a gift-horse in the mouth. I wouldn't consider mounting – much less buying – any horse without getting a good vet to look at its teeth.'

He smiled discreetly. 'Spoken like a true Endel, Rose – but as to why she chose you, I can only presume for the obvious reason that she wished you to have it. And from what John Watson told me this morning –' he took a handwritten sheet of foolscap from the open file on his desk – 'she was of sound mind and in good health for her age when she called into his office three months ago, instructed him to draw up her will and subsequently signed it in the presence of his chief clerk and himself.'

My mind flipped up a name. 'Frank Cross.'

He raised both eyebrows. 'You're well informed.'

'Not particularly. It's just that Duncan's Consort has kept coming into my life recently. He's their bass.'

'Don't remind me.' He looked up at the exquisitely proportioned high ceiling in mock horror. 'Charlotte detests madrigals and I'm tone-deaf, but as Maria Gillon has insisted to Charlotte that everyone who is anyone will be at tomorrow's concert and Maria's presidency of the Cliffhill Floral Society must end in September and Charlotte – how shall I put it? – has much enjoyed being vice-president, we have two front stalls. Of course, you'll be there.'

'If David's up to it.'

He nodded. We had already dealt with David's health and PC Parker's frustrations. 'If you can make it I may have the keys of Ferry Cottage for you. The only spare set is due to be returned to John Watson's office tomorrow morning. He's taking his wife to the concert and hopes to hand me the keys. You can't take possession until after probate but he has no objection to your looking the property over at your own convenience once it has been cleared. Should you not make the concert I'll register the keys to you on Monday.'

'Thanks. No hurry. I've never been inside Ferry but from the outside it needs repairing before it can be rented or sold. As I haven't yet had time to think what I'll do with it, so far I've only told David she's left it to me.'

'Very prudent. One hint would be enough to have the marsh grapevine agog with speculations.' He smiled self-derisively. 'Though that frequently irritated me in my youth, I have rather missed it since we moved to Astead. We have pleasant neighbours but none with the ability to tell us what everyone in our road is doing at every hour of the day and night.' He paused a few moments. 'Odd that no one in St Martin's should have seen anything of Dr Lofthouse's assailant.'

'Only in one way, Edward.' Our eyes met. 'Parker's still insisting it was an outside job.'

'Parker knows his patch.' He looked down at the open file. 'However, to return to the matter in hand . . .'

We discussed technicalities for a little longer then he saw me down to the office car park behind the house. My car was a hot oven, and he helped open all the windows. 'I appreciate your anxiety to return to your invalid,' he said in farewell, 'but drive carefully. With this heat forecast to last into next week, London'll be emptying for a weekend by the sea.'

The southbound traffic was nose to tail on the newish clearway that connected the main London and coast roads, south of Astead. As the long way back to Midstreet would almost certainly be the quickest, nine miles on I turned off into a narrow lane that wound drunkenly over a stretch of moorland and ended at an ancient stone bridge over a main dyke. The bridge was too narrow for vans and tractors and had been built long before the Ditch had been dug and when that stretch had already been named Fishers Moor, after the 'night fishermen', that is, smugglers, who for centuries had used it as the shortest land route to Astead from the marsh. It was reputed to be haunted by the ghosts of three eighteenth-century Excise men found lying in the lane with their throats cut.

I had never seen or known anyone who had seen those ghosts, but I knew many who still refused to cross Fishers Moor at night. In the hot noon sunshine with the sky alive with birds, the shorn sheep drowsily grazing the rough-cropped common land, the banks of the lane mosaics of bluebells, buttercups, dandelions and cow parsley, it was easy to dismiss old legend as superstitious nonsense. Not so easy on a moonless winter night with a mist coming up from the marsh, distorting shapes and sounds and reducing visibility to a few feet or inches. According to legend the Excise men had been murdered on such a moonless misty winter night, their murderers had never been found and no one had seen or heard anything that might have hinted at their identity. 'Watch the wall, my darling, while the Gentlemen go by,' I reflected, slowing to crawl the car over the old bridge, had been marsh tradition centuries before Kipling wrote 'A Smuggler's Song'.

I was still pursuing that thought when I drove through the main gates. Half-way up the drive I saw Marlene leaning out of my office window and beckoning me to the front of Endel. God, now what? I speeded and skidded to a stop by the mounting-block and Jody barked wildly from somewhere indoors. I leapt out, bellowing, 'Relax, Jody! I'm back.' The barking stopped. 'What's up, Marlene?'

'Rats is back, Miss Rose! Don't take your car round the yard!' Her face was flushed with excitement. 'Mr

86

Lofthouse and Murdo gone after 'em and Mr Lofthouse said to keep Jody in as they'll be putting down poison.'

'Oh, God, not again!' I flopped against the car, torn between my terror of rats and relief for David. Then I realised what else she had said. 'Mr Lofthouse shouldn't be ratting in this heat.'

Marlene flung up her arms. 'I couldn't stop him, miss. You know what the men are with rats.'

'Yes. God knows why.' I shuddered. 'I'd better investigate.'

'Rather you than me, miss.' She backed in and closed the window.

Nervously I walked round to the yard where a large flagstone had been prised up and David and Murdo were on their knees peering into the exposed cavity. David wore a broad-brimmed panama hat I had not seen before and two pairs of glasses that when he glanced up hid the now brownish-yellow smudges beneath his eyes. 'No rats *in situ*, Rose. Take a look at this.'

Murdo's capped head jerked up. 'You do that, ma'am, or you'll nae credit my words.'

I nerved myself, went close and gasped. The cavity had been neatly tunnelled and in tidy little heaps on the earthen floor were bulbs scraped clean of soil. 'Murdo, aren't those autumn crocuses.'

'Aye.' He was very angry. 'Three hundred I planted down the drive beds last week. Three hundred, I'm telling you – and this forenoon I thought to take a look at the few to see how they were coming along. The topsoil was that smooth you'd think it not touched since my rake but when I took my fork to the beds – not the one left! I was putting my mind to who could have taken them when Mr Lofthouse came out and observed the few wee holes no

87

bigger than a skewer would make and said, maybe rats. We searched all about and then observed the fresh chippings down the sides of yon flag and had it up.' He jerked a thumb downwards. 'My bulbs!'

I said, 'If I hadn't seen this I couldn't have believed even rats could be so clever.'

'Never underestimate their intelligence, Rose.' David stood up and wiped his hands on his denims. 'That's their secret weapon.'

'That's a fact.' Murdo heaved himself upright. 'The crafty wee –' he hesitated – 'beasties kent fine what they were about. But they'll nae be filling their bellies with my bulbs. I'll have the lot away and sort the beasties.' He glared at me. 'I'll mind to lock away the poison when I'm done and you best be out this yard for the day. It'll be nae place for a woman.' He shuffled off mumbling to himself.

David hitched his hat brim to nudge his glasses. 'He'll finish them off.'

'I know.' I flattened a hand above my eyes and looked up at what I could see of his still faintly yellowish and too taut face. 'Just the thought they are around gives me the horrors. Another of my hang-ups,' I added as we began walking back to the house. He still walked like an old man.

He said absently, 'It's no hang-up to dislike the sensation that somewhere close there's an alien intelligence working against one. How was Astead?'

'Hot. I'll give you the lowdown inside. You shouldn't hang around in this heat.'

'Cooler than Washington and less humidity,' he retorted dismissively. 'Have I time to shower off the rats before lunch?'

'Sure. No hurry. It's cold.'

'Thanks. With you shortly.' He walked ahead quickly and had just passed the main kitchen window when he stopped, swayed slightly, then went on much more slowly. Only the sight of Marlene and Daph at the kitchen window prevented my rushing after him.

They catapulted out of the back door. Daph gasped, 'He nearly crumpled, Miss Rose!'

'So I saw.' They were my friends as well as helps. 'I let him be, as he wouldn't want to know that.'

'Same as my hubby,' said Marlene. 'Can't abide being fussed.'

Daph said she was lucky. 'My Ted can't have enough. Cold in the head and he thinks he's going. But Mr Lofthouse isn't right yet, miss.'

'Or has just been out in this sun too long.' I sounded more sanguine than I felt. 'You off, now?'

They exchanged glances. Marlene said, 'Don't seem right leaving you.'

'Thanks, but if necessary I'll bulldoze Mr Lofthouse back to bed and ring the doctor. But, first – about the rats . . .'

My news cheered them. 'Well, I never! They never! Did you ever? . . . Well, seeing as you say – see you in the morning, miss.'

I went back into the flat determined to ring Maria and cancel our date when she should be home between meetings after lunch. 'The traffic was hellish this morning,' I told David at lunch. 'Can't say I fancy it this afternoon.'

He gave me a straight look. 'I know you mean well, Rosie –'

'And a more damning thing you can't say –'

'Precisely. So stop reminding me I'm a bloody alba-tross or I'm off for the first fast from Astead once we've stacked the dishwasher.'

I felt happier. 'Why not Gatwick?'

'A: I don't fancy spending the weekend yo-yoing across the Atlantic. B: We haven't yet sorted out whether I'm staying.'

'Other matters on our minds.'

'Just the one or two.' He tilted his head at Jody sprawled panting across the open dining-room doorway. 'Have to leave *in situ*?'

I nodded. 'Feeling like Judas.'

He gave a queer little grimace. 'Par for the course. I'll get the coffee.'

The coast-bound traffic was even heavier than in the morning but as we were going against it, apart from one omission I gave him a detailed account of my session with Edward. I should have known better.

'What was his reaction to your slapping the paternity suit on Grandad?'

I smiled faintly. 'Same as yours.'

'But that hasn't reassured you.'

'Probably as I can't see straight for chips. What did Julian say about you this morning?'

'That he wished he had more patients like me, was sorry to miss you, looks forward to seeing us both at tomorrow's concert and his old man's on and he's off for the weekend from this evening.' There was an artificial smile in his voice. 'Buddy-buddies are Jule and I. How to make friends and influence people – get your brains spilled out of your ears.'

I glanced sideways. 'Drop the act, David. This is me, remember?'

'I haven't forgotten, love,' he said and fell silent until we reached Littlemarsh and saw a navy saloon parked on the grass verge of the cross-dyke that fronted Ferry Cottage. 'I know that job.'

'Looks like the Blacks' Allegro.'

'Let's find out.' He put and kept his hand on the horn while I drew over and braked just ahead of the parked car. Before I switched off the engine Sandra charged from the low front door and over the rickety wooden bridge, shouting furiously, 'If you're wondering what I'm doing I've the owner's written permission – oh! It's you! My God, David – you look ghastly! No wonder Duncan's still got the shakes! Frightfully sorry to bawl you out but I thought you were just being nosy and was about to brandish Chrissie's note and her solicitor's letter.' She misinterpreted our fascinated silence. 'Chrissie's not actually the new owner of the place, but the old bag left her all her furniture and clothes and things. Rather sweet of her, actually.'

David and I chorused, 'Very.' I added, 'Christine told me they'd hit it off in the General.'

'God, haven't we heard! All her patients adore her, she says – just like Harry! His boss is lending him a van to shift the lot this evening to a lock-up garage in Coxden Chrissie's scrounged from another ex-patient. Does she beat all at twisting arms – including mine. That's why I'm here. She asked me to look things over in case the valuer missed something good.' She shrugged disparagingly. 'She should be so lucky! Every stick of furniture's riddled with woodworm – all the old bits of china are jumble-sale fodder – rows of hideous toby jugs – but there is one rather pretty smallboy that might be worth treating, polishing up and sending to auction. I was trying to prise it from the wall when I heard you. Weighs a ton.'

'I'll give you a hand, Sandra.' David was out of the car as fast as on Tuesday evening. 'Rose has a date but I'm just along for the ride.'

'David, thanks awfully – but, Rose – should he?'

I spread my hands. 'Probably not. I can't stop him.'

'Just like Steve! He never takes any notice of anything I say when he's ill. Not that he often is. Chrissie says that's because I'm so lousy with sick people. She's always holding forth about understanding the psychology of her patients. Ha!' She snorted maliciously. 'She wasn't so hot on the old bag's! She hasn't said, but Steve and I are sure she hoped she'd be left the cottage. She doesn't know who has – solicitors are so cagey – but I'll bet it's someone who's an even better smarmer than Chrissie.'

I had been about to enlighten her. I changed my mind. 'Open question.'

David slapped the car roof. 'What isn't, is that Maria'll blow fuses if you don't shift, Rose. I'll follow on.'

'Right. Cheers, Sandra.' I drove on slowly and in the driving mirror watched them cross the bridge and David crouch to follow Sandra inside. Until that moment I had not given the cottage itself one thought. I discovered I didn't need thought to know I neither liked nor wanted it. I disliked still more leaving David, but as that was what he patently wanted I hoped he knew what he was doing. He generally did, I reflected, driving on uneasily.

Old Nora was waiting for me in the front garden of Potts House. She wore the long-sleeved, navy nylon button-through that was her 'afternoon' uniform and though she looked sad and lonely there was a new vitality about her. 'Mrs Henry's just rung from the vicarage to say she's sorry she'll be a little late and I'm to make you a nice cup of tea, Miss Rose.' She ushered me into the darkly panelled and carpeted front hall that smelt of must, wax polish and Brasso and was dim after the sunshine outside. 'But I'm ever so glad to see you private, miss. I got something ever so nice to tell you! Her ladyship – rest her good, kind soul – left me two hundred pounds a year long as I live!'

'Nora!' I hugged her. 'I'm so glad.'

'And that's not all, miss!' She shook her head in wonder. 'Mr Henry wants me to stay on caretaking on full wages, bed and board, till he and Mrs Henry decides what's to be done – could take months, he says – and then he'll pay all my expenses when I move down Hastings to my sister, Amy. And Mrs Henry's given me so many of her ladyship's lovely clothes neither me nor Amy'll need to buy more till our time comes! But I mustn't keep you standing out here. If you'll just step into the drawing room I'll fetch in your tea. I got the kettle on.'

'Couldn't we have it in the kitchen? I want to hear more about Amy. I'm ashamed to say I never knew you had any family.'

'Just Amy, miss, and you wouldn't know of her seeing Master Rosser wasn't weaned when Amy married a Sussex chap and moved down Hastings to his mum, seeing he gone for a soldier in the Great War.' She was so delighted by the prospect of prolonging this conversation that I felt as much a Judas as when leaving Jody. 'Sure you'll not mind the kitchen? I don't know what Mrs Henry'll say.'

'I'll tell her,' I insisted. I went ahead through the old green baize swing door at the back of the hall and down

93

the narrow corridor to the large, stone-flagged, old-fashioned kitchen that had a window overlooking the kitchen garden and Ferry Cottage beyond. As I walked over to it, David and Sandra emerged from the front door and after a brief, smiling exchange Sandra ducked back inside and David crossed the bridge and road and stood looking down at the main dyke.

'Milk and no sugar, isn't it, miss?'

'Please.' I joined her at the white-scrubbed table on which stood a bowl of cornflowers that matched the blue of the Victorian delft kitchen crockery. I sat facing the window. 'Did Amy work in Endel, Nora?'

'Oh, yes, miss. Head nursery-maid she was and lovely with kiddies. Shame she never had none – but I don't reckon she was too sorry, seeing her hubby come back from the war gassed bad and couldn't do another day's work and gone three years later.'

'Oh, poor Amy!'

She nodded reminiscently. 'Bad time she had, but could've been a sight worse if his old mum'd not been a proper cook and learned Amy to cook proper. So Amy gone into service cooking and never had the day out of the place till she picked up her pension. Still cooking the two days a week for one of her ladies for all she's the year older than me.'

'Good for Amy.' David had begun strolling towards the foot of the hill. 'Did you see much of her in Endel?'

'Times, I did, times I didn't, miss. Her ladyship – Mrs Arthur, she was then – always fetched me with her when staying with Mrs Endel – your grandma, dear – and when Master Rosser was coming we was there ever so long. Well, I mean –' she refilled our cups – 'having a bad time with Master Richard, Mrs Endel was nervous, like, and needed the bit of company seeing Mr Endel was up and down London seeing to the war.' She pursed her lips. 'Like the monthly nurse as come down from London told Amy – can't expect a gentleman to understand and when a lady's time come it's not her gentleman she needs but her doctor. Now what was her name?' She paused. 'Hicks? No! Why did I say that? Oh, I know – that Nurse Hicks put me in mind of her. Nurse Sumers, she was, and another proper little madam. But ever so good – and gone afore the year was out.'

'Gone?' David had stopped for another look at the main dyke. 'You mean from Endel?'

She looked at me with the indulgence she would have shown a retarded child. 'Oh no, dear. Like I said, she was a monthly, and after she left Endel she gone to nurse our boys in France and gone the seven months later. Same as too many. Her ladyship see her name in the casualty lists. Cruel those lists were. Day after day, so many gone, young and younger than that Nurse Sumers.' She glanced round at the window. 'Both Mercer boys gone on the Somme the same day. Twenty-one and nineteen.'

I forgot David. 'Ginny's brothers?' She nodded. 'Nora – how hideous! I never even knew she had had brothers, though I heard her fiancé was killed.'

'Cruel war and cruel time for many, it was. Don't do to brood on it and don't help to talk. Not that she was much of a talker.' Her sniff reminded me of Daph's on Saturday morning. 'All these years she never give me more than the time of day. Thought herself too good for the likes of me for all she was no better than she should be.' She realised what she had just said and added hastily, 'Leastways, so they said.'

I said quietly, 'So I've heard. I suppose there was a lot of talk.'

Nora looked down her nose. 'A girl as gets herself in trouble can't expect no other, miss.'

'I suppose not, particularly when conventions were so much stricter than now. Did the baby live?'

She looked up and her eyes glazed over. 'Couldn't say, I'm sure, miss. There was some as said it was a nice little lad with her fair hair and blue eyes and got put out for adoption. There was others as said the Lord took back what wasn't wanted. I can't tell you who said rightly. I never heard her ladyship speak of it and I knew my place better than to ask. Couldn't abide dirty talk, her ladyship couldn't, unlike some I could – oh!' The front doorbell interrupted and perturbed her. 'Who'll that be? Mrs Henry just walks in, and door's open.'

I jumped up. 'Probably for me. I'll deal with it.' I vanished before she could protest, and heard her hurrying after me. When I opened the unlocked front door David was on the doorstep and Maria racing up the path behind him. David was wearing his normal glasses and she was appalled by his appearance. 'Darling, you look a positive wreck!'

He smiled, 'You should have seen me a couple of days ago, Maria. No, thanks, I won't come in. I only looked in to say I'm not stopping as I know you girls are going to be busy.' He looked at me. 'I feel like a walk. Look out for me on the home run and if you're not done 'till after opening time your best bet'll be on one of the benches outside the Lamb.'

Maria protested: 'It's three miles to Coxden. Far too far.'

'Worth the try. If necessary I'll collapse on the left

verge, Rose. Don't work too hard, girls.' And again he walked away like an old man.

Maria frowned at his back and whispered, 'Stop him, Rose. He'll never make it.'

I said under my breath, 'Or thank me for bashing his ego by saying so in public.'

She sighed, 'I suppose not. Men are such fools and anyway, he's not your husband. Had tea? Good. Let's get cracking as it's going to be hell.'

It was.

When I drove by Ferry three hours later the Allegro had been replaced by a smallish white van and through the open front door of the cottage I glimpsed Harry's back. There was no sign of David on the road to Coxden or on the crowded benches outside the Lamb, but when I crossed Coxden bridge I saw him sitting against an old milestone on the narrow grass verge between the road and the nearside dyke. He sat with his arms folded and legs outstretched and looked so relaxed that I thought him asleep until I was close enough to see he was watching two swans languidly circling in the dyke. I touched the horn, signalled to the car behind and stopped with my foot down on the clutch and engine running. He got in quickly and I apologised for taking so long. 'Get a beer?'

'Didn't bother. You look as if you could use one.'

'Not right now, thanks.' He was not a heavy drinker but that he hadn't fancied a pint on a hot evening was unhealthy, as was his now adding his dark glasses though the sun was behind us. 'You just been sitting watching swans?'

'On and off. I paced that pair from Littlemarsh. They'd gone far as they wanted to go and so had I.' He

97

jerked a thumb at his window. 'Where does this dyke drain?'

'Via a few cross-dykes into Midstreet main and under the wall into the sea.' I checked the driving-mirror then glanced at him. He wasn't smoking and even his powerful shoulders sagged. What I had prised out of Nora, and the fact that she and Maria had spent the last three hours in floods of tears, could wait. 'What's Ferry like inside?'

'Primitive, but neat as hell, despite the omnipresence of dry rot and rising damp. The living room's too small to swing a cat but has a hearth that takes up most of the chimney wall, there's a minute upstairs bedroom and a back slit of a kitchen with a mains cold tap, hip-bath under the sink and aged Calor gas cooker. Plus outside privy.'

'And cellar?'

He turned to me. 'I didn't see it and Sandra didn't mention it. Has it got one?'

I thought back. 'I'm not sure. I just thought there must be a cellar as most old buildings of its age have them and Ginny Mercer once told me she could store apples six months and still have them worth eating raw. I assumed she kept them in her cellar. She could have kept them in her loft. Did you smell apples?'

'Just dry rot, rising damp and scouring-powder.' He was quiet for a few minutes. 'She liked her home, Rosie. Could be why she wanted you to have it. She knew you can afford to put it in good order.'

'You honestly think so?'

Again he forced a smile into his voice. 'With what I've got functioning in that department. Yes.'

'Headache giving you hell?'

'Not particularly.'

98

'Rubbish. Sooner you're back in bed with a couple of aspirins the better.'

'Christ, Lofthouse are you bloody washed-up! All she now thinks you need in bed is a couple of bloody analgesics.'

'Cool it, chum. I just think you need another early night. And you know I'm right.'

He didn't answer at once. Then: 'On one condition. No supper-tray. We eat together then I opt out and you can get back to the unfinished business that Murdo says had your typewriter going at five this morning. Deal?'

'Yes,' I said gratefully. I still had over two hours' work waiting in my office. 'And thanks.'

'For bloody what?'

'For being the only man I know, aside from Walt, that takes my work seriously.'

He grunted as if that gave him no joy and neither of us said more until we were back in Endel.

We had just finished supper when Walt rang, ostensibly to tell me the new tractor had arrived this afternoon and in reality to know we were back alive. 'Just been another pile-up on the Ditch road the mite south of Coxden bridge, madam. Nasty one, seemly. Five private cars, the one towing a caravan that's gone into the Ditch, a milk lorry and a van. The Old Doctor's been fetched out and ambulances and fire engines from Cliffhill. Firemen needed to cut 'em out.'

I had taken the call in the office. I sat on the desk and closed my eyes. My mother and stepfather of eighteen months had been killed in a motorway pile-up two months before I married Charles. 'Walt, I'm so sorry – we must've just missed . . . Those poor people! And always happening, summer weekends.'

'I just said as much to my wife, madam. Mind you, I'm glad as you missed it. Mr Lofthouse the better for his outing?'

'Not much.'

'Nah. Done too much, I shouldn't wonder. When I stepped by the Crown for my pint old Murdo said as Mr Lofthouse not done himself too much good ratting. He may sleep the better for it. 'Night, madam.'

David had cleared the dining-room table and was stacking the dishwasher. He glanced round and hitched down his glasses. 'Why's Walt turned you a dirty shade of green?'

'Another pile-up.' I repeated Walt's account. 'I should be used to them by now. There's one somewhere on the marsh every weekend in the holiday season. Happening to people on hols somehow makes it worse. They think the marsh and the dykes look so pretty and harmless and don't realise country roads can be far more dangerous than motorways. Still –' I shrugged – 'nothing we can do about it. Thanks for doing all this. I'll finish off.' He blinked at me and propped his knuckles on his hips. Suddenly, I exploded, 'For God's sake, man, lay off and get to bed! Don't you realise I'm worried crazy about you?'

'It had crossed my mind, love.' He pulled off his glasses, took me in his arms and kissed me, tenderly. 'I'll finish off then go quietly if you'll do something for me?'

'Like what?'

'Like getting straight into your office and down to the job that keeps the roof on Endel and a couple of dozen full-time workers off the dole queues.'

'Right.' I kissed him. 'Sleep well.'

He kissed me in answer.

It was nearly eleven when I got wearily out of my desk chair and filed the invoices and books in the largest filing cabinet. Jody had been sprawled asleep across the foot of the closed door. She stood up and shook herself, then stiffened with her ears up for the split-second before David called quietly. 'OK to intrude?'

I forgot I was dog-tired. 'Yes. Shift, Jody – can't you sleep?'

'Otherwise occupied. Thanks.' I opened the door and he came in with a small tray loaded with an unopened bottle of whisky, a soda siphon, bowl of ice cubes and two glasses. He had showered and shaved, wore clean cream cotton pyjamas under his dressing-gown and looked refreshed and infinitely stronger than when I had left him in the kitchen. He put the tray on the desk. 'I knew you had finished when I heard you closing the filing cabinet. I thought you rated a short one and it was time we used one of my duty-frees. And then,' he touched the strapping on the back of his head, 'you can tell me specifically why you are convinced this was on target and I'll tell you why I think there's a high degree of probability that you are right. After which, my love,' he went on in a different tone, 'I hope we can get to bed. I don't know what my self-denying ordinance has been doing to you, but I'll tell you straight, it's bloody killing me.' He opened the whisky. 'Straight, drowned or on the rocks?'

SIX

J<small>ODY'S</small> <small>BARKING WOKE US BEFORE WE HEARD THE</small> approaching motorbike. David fumbled for his watch on my bedside table. 'Five to seven. Parker?'

'Mushrooms,' I muttered, sleepily. The second half of the night had been a glory, but short on sleep. I yelled, 'Kevin, Jody!' She stopped barking and we heard her streaking to the front door. Still only half awake I sat up. 'Where's my kaftan? Thanks.' I hauled it over my head. 'They're coming up now in our private wood and I've said he can help himself. He drops off my danegeld on his way to work Saturdays and flogs the rest to the general stores in Coxden.' The motorbike engine cut out and my bedside telephone rang.

'I'll take Kev.' David passed me the receiver and dived out of bed for his pyjamas on the floor. We detested sleeping with the curtains closed and the open window faced east; in the early sunshine the scars were a white trellis on his tanned back.

'Rose? That you?' demanded Duncan's tinny voice from under my chin.

I reversed the receiver. 'Yes – sorry, Duncan. Not properly awake. Good morning.'

'Good? How can you say that after –' and the rest was drowned by Jody's ecstatic response to the ringing doorbell. She loved Kevin.

'Just a moment, Duncan.' I covered the mouthpiece and smiled at David. 'He's bugged this room.'

He grinned. 'Tonight I sweep it first.' He grabbed his dressing-gown and vanished. I waited till he had quietened Jody and heard Kevin's 'Blimey, Mr Lofthouse, what's the other guy look like?' then uncovered the mouthpiece. 'Sorry about that, Duncan. What were you saying?'

'You haven't heard?' He sounded outraged.

'Jody deafened me and –'

'Not that! That nightmare of a pile-up that should never have happened! I was sure Walt Ames had told you. The police must've contacted his wretched brother last night. His van caused it. He must've known the brakes were faulty and should be charged with criminal negligence!'

I was wide awake. 'The one on the Ditch road?'

'You had heard!'

'Only that there'd been one. Have Harry and Christine –'

'Just Harry – that poor boy – my tenor – Chrissie says multiple head and chest injuries.'

'Oh God.' I closed my eyes. 'How?'

'How can I bear to tell you? But –' he gave a long, shuddering sigh, 'I must. Chrissie said the van went out of control and skidded broadside into an oncoming milk

103

lorry that jacknifed and got the cars coming both ways. I've forgotten how many, but one had an empty caravan that went into the Ditch. Chrissie said the police told her there was brake fluid all over the road. Obviously faulty brakes!'

'How many injured? Killed? And how's Chrissie?'

He ignored all but my last question. 'One can only thank whatever gods there be that her off-duty was changed and she wasn't with him. If not, I would have to cancel our concert. How could I find a first soprano at such short notice? As it is,' he wailed, 'I've had to spend most of the night making new arrangements. I've had to scrap the countertenor as I must take tenor. How will I sing a note?'

His egocentricity would have appalled me far more if I had not married a writer. If Charles when working had managed to survive an H-bomb dropped overhead his only reaction would have been fury at the interruption. I clucked soothingly as I had learned to cluck to Charles, then asked, 'Why was Harry on the Ditch road? That's the long way to Cliffhill from Littlemarsh.'

'He was off at six and Chrissie had to work till eight so they decided he would start shifting this stuff she's been left – but Sandra told you all that.'

'Yes. Go on.'

He gave another long sigh. 'Yes, well – Harry had just taken the first load to some empty garage in Coxden and was returning to Cliffhill to collect Chrissie and finish the clearing together. She was just going off duty when the police rang the hospital warning they were bringing in fifteen road casualties and that six were seriously injured. She had to volunteer to stay on – it's not a big hospital – and was in casualty when they were carried in. She – so brave, dear child – rang me soon as she could, but that wasn't till nearly midnight. She said Harry was in coma – no! I can't talk about him! I can't dwell on personal grief – I've got to concentrate on tonight. I mustn't disappoint our public!'

'You won't, Duncan.'

'You're such a strength, Rose! That's why I just had to ring you before leaving for Cliffhill. We must rehearse this morning and Chrissie said my only hope of getting her the extra time off is to see her matron – or whatever she's now called – in person shortly after she comes on duty at eight. There's so much to do that only I can deal with. Why, oh why, should all this be happening to me?'

My marriage had taught me that answer too. 'Poor Duncan. You're having a very tough streak.'

'You always understand. You will be with us tonight?' he demanded urgently. 'Never have we more desperately needed the support of all our friends.'

My God, I thought, this is really why you've rung me. And in your place, so would Charles. 'You'll have it. Do tell the others and particularly Christine how very sorry I am about Harry and for you all.'

'Bless you.' He rang off.

A few minutes earlier I had heard Kevin leaving, and from the quiet in the flat David and Jody were still outside. I knew I should get up. On Saturdays normally Walt sealed the farm post in a foolscap envelope and sent it down, but he would bring it this morning. I lay back and listened to the chattering house martins under the roof, the cries of the gulls, the murmuring sea, the distant rumble of tractors and hay-bailers starting work and the voices in my mind. Duncan's just now; Maria's on the evening Maud Gillon died; David's and mine in the office last night. And it was only then that I realised how much I had told him and how little he had told me.

Jody had gone back to sleep across the foot of the closed door when David said, 'I've known from Wednesday morning that you'd decided I was the intended target, but as you had been wrong about that in the past, my initial reaction was that you were just stuck in the old groove. But as my mind was still hazy as hell I thought I'd tread water, play it your way, let one and all know I was a dead loss and see what, if anything, turned up.'

'I collected Ferry.'

'How do you fit that into your pattern?'

'I can't. Yet. I've just got a vague feeling that it does, somehow. But I'm not vague – I'm sure you were clouted to get you out of the action for the rest of your hols. You're too good at smelling out rats and too thick with Sir Norman Hurst for the comfort of person or persons unknown.' We were sitting in my swivel chair and I gently fingered the still ugly lump over his left temple. 'I don't know what you had to be stopped from rumbling, but as he got you in Duncan's cottage, could be that Duncan's involved. You mayn't remember this, but it was his grabbing my shoulder that prevented my charging after you in time to see who was nipping out to his kitchen.'

'I do remember. Near total recall now.' He thought a moment. 'If his hysteria was an act, he's missed his trade. He knocks spots off Olivier. But his cottage is clean. Murdo told me this morning the cops toothcombed it Tuesday night and again Wednesday morning.'

'Then why do you now think I might be right about why you, personally, got it?'

'The silence, love.'

'Yes,' I said unhappily. 'He's not just marsh, he's local marsh, so St Martin's is watching the wall. I'll bet Parker knows this and is just plugging the outsider angle to get someone sufficiently off-guard, or drunk enough, to blurt out something. Parker's problem is that, like you, he's a foreigner. I wish to God the sod had clouted me.'

His arms tightened round me. 'I bloody don't.'

'Only because you don't know Walt like I do. The old feudal system's long defunct but it lives on in him. Clobbering his thane would have him out for blood and the four Ames brothers cover a lot of territory and carry a lot of clout.'

'Oh, aye.' He frowned as if there was something he was trying to remember. I held my mental breath until he said 'Four? I thought five.'

'Not since John, the third, was killed in the war. He wasn't married, but the others are and they're still very close-knit. Walt, the oldest, was about seven when their father died and has been head of the family since he was out of short pants. When old Mrs Ames died in St Martin's last year, half the marsh and hordes from Coxden and Cliffhill came to her funeral.' I thought back. 'Duncan wore a black bow-tie.'

'Not the mothball suiting?'

I shook my head. 'I only saw him in that on Tuesday. Mean anything?'

'Probably no more than that he knows his public.'

I thought aloud: 'And having spent most of the war in the army, how to bugger his own wiring?'

He smiled quietly, 'You don't let go easy, love.'

'Nor do you. Care to tell me why you were so eager to

get inside Ferry and why so sold on swans this after-noon?'

'Just plain curiosity, and I've always liked swans.'

'And were only academically interested in finding out if it's possible to get from Littlemarsh to the sea by dyke?'

'Still playing it your way.'

'Huh?'

'Yes. You smelt smugglers with that first mothball. When I looked round Littlemarsh it struck me that were this possible it would be a very handy spot for a nice quiet nocturnal delivery. The only two dwelling-houses anywhere near the main dyke have been occupied for years by three elderly ladies. The elderly tend to have impaired vision and often, hearing, and to go to bed early.'

Again I thought aloud: 'And two of the three are now dead.'

He groaned. 'Hold on, desist. Pray, stop! No murders tonight or I shall weep piteously on your shoulder. My heart is impure, my strength faileth and I need my bed. And by Christ, love,' he added in another voice, 'do I need you.'

David came in with the tea. He had put the mushrooms in the fridge, left Jody with Murdo and had his and Kevin's reports of the pile-up. I gave him Duncan's. 'But the show must go on.'

'Yes.' He took his mug to the window and stood with his back to it. 'Why didn't Walt give you the whole picture last night?'

'Not my problem and I suspect Mrs Walt was in range. Walt reckons a man's problems are strictly a man's business.'

'Like my dad. My mum's spent her married life sorting them for him without his catching on. Mrs Walt do that?'

I smiled. 'Anything but. She's too thick to recognise a problem if she saw one. So's John, though he looks an outsize Walt. Kevin's the reverse.'

'Looks a smart lad.' He looked into his mug as if reading the tea-leaves. 'If those brakes prove faulty, George'll have a problem.'

'And Duncan if they aren't and he doesn't stop slinging criminal negligence at George. The whole Ames family'll gang up against him. Couldn't it just have been fair wear and tear?'

He was mesmerised by the tea-leaves. 'One probability.'

I looked more closely at his downcast face and a trickle of ice ran down my spine. 'What are the others?'

He looked up but wasn't seeing me. 'Insufficient data to formulate even a provisional hypothesis.'

'Which means you're wondering if someone fixed those brakes to fail.'

'Why would anyone risk what later transpired just to get even with George or Harry or both?'

'Stakes high enough to be worth that risk?'

He blinked and saw me. 'If that's right he's a ruthless, lethally dangerous sod.'

'Like the one that could've killed you. Two around?' He didn't answer. 'How do you fix brakes to fail?'

'Several ways. Far the quickest is to get under with a large pair of pliers and squeeze the brake pipes. Once they give, fluid drains out and the brakes seize up.'

'How quick? Minutes?'

'Seconds, if you know what you're doing.'

I thought of Littlemarsh last evening. 'Then it could easily have been done outside Ferry when Harry was packing up inside. Maria, Nora and I had been working in the front bedroom for hours. The van was outside when I drove by but I hadn't seen it earlier.' He nodded absently and I got out of bed. 'Switch off the computer for a second. Mushrooms fried or grilled?'

'Oh – neither, thanks. I've gone off mushrooms since my last lot in the States kicked back sharpish. I'll fix breakfast. Fried for you, isn't it?' he added, forgetting I loathed cooked breakfasts.

'Not this morning. Just toast.'

We breakfasted together, but he was only with me physically. He had taken Jody for a run on the beach when the helps and Walt arrived. Marlene bristled with ruffled family pride – her husband was Mrs George Ames's second cousin – but Walt, blindingly white-shirted, looked his usual calm self. He did accept an office chair. 'Don't mind if I do, madam.'

We dealt with farm business first. Then I told him Duncan had rung me. 'Was it the brakes, Walt?'

'If it was, madam, my brother George can't say for why, seeing he had young Harry give the van the extra check yesterday morning.' He sat straight-backed, his large, hard hands on his short, thick thighs, his eyes steady. 'George'll not hire out nor lend any vehicle without the extra check and said as much to the cops up Cliffhill last night. Nothing they could say till their forensics had the look. They'll not have an easy job seeing the van's scrap metal.'

I winced. 'Miracle Harry survived.'

'Aye.' I just glimpsed the flare of anger in his eyes before he looked down at his hands. 'Upset George, this has. Steady lad and good fitter as never skimped a job, George reckons Harry.' He looked back at me. 'Mind you, like I said to George, always a first time.'

'Always. Do you think that's what may have happened?'

'Too early to say, madam. We'll sort it out.'

I accepted the warning. 'Yes. Far too early. But I am so sorry for you about all this.'

'You don't have to tell me, madam. Much obliged, mind.' He looked at the window behind me. 'Nice as Mr Lofthouse is up to running Jody today.'

'Very, though he still looks battered.'

'Can't wonder after that nasty blow. Will he be off to the concert with you tonight?'

'I hope so –' I smiled faintly – 'though I'm not sure he does. He's not sold on madrigals.'

A faint smile flickered in Walt's eyes. 'Same as me and my wife, madam. Can't abide all that fancy singing, so when Mr Morgan comes round with his tickets my wife says she's ever so sorry but fixed special to visit her sister up Shepland tonight. I'll not be with her as her brother-in-law's got bell-ringers' practice. I'll have it nice and quiet with me telly and me dogs.' He reached for his hat. 'Will that be all?'

I thought fast. He needed an anodyne and I needed to clear one of the most persistent black patches in my mental pattern. 'Not if you can spare a few more minutes.' He slapped the hat on his lap. 'I haven't yet explained why I had to see Mr Edward Smith yesterday. Ginny Mercer's left me Ferry Cottage.'

'You don't say, madam!' I had never seen him openly astounded. 'I heard as she'd taken a bit of a fancy to you, but I never reckoned on this.' His rare smile relaxed his red face and would have relieved me if it had not contained an element of almost triumphant relief. 'Mind you, from what young Kevin says it's a wonder it's still standing, but after you got a good builder on the job it could be a nice little windfall. And first bit of Endel property on the mainland.'

I was touched by his genuine and unconsciously feudal pleasure. The Endels had provided him and his innumerable forefathers with their livings. Endel pride was his pride, which was why I could never offend him by asking him for the truth about Ginny's baby. I smiled. 'A dodgy bit. I've heard it reeks of dry rot and rising damp. I've never been inside. Has Kevin?'

'Times, seemly, since he been working for Mr Matthews. Old Ginny fetched him in for a quick cuppa on and off, he says. Mind you, she been all over him since he was a nipper. She never gave my wife and John more than a nod, but had a nice word for me when we met up Coxden Fair August Bank Holidays.' He wagged his bullet-shaped head. 'No offence, madam, but never any saying for why with womenfolks' fancies.'

I laughed. 'Nor need to where Kevin's concerned.'

He scowled to cover his paternal pride. He loved John, but adored Kevin. 'That cocky young shaver'll not hear that from me. Head's big enough without. Thinks he knows it all and won't be told.'

Something stirred in my mind but before I could identify it my telephone started ringing. 'Excuse me. Wait –'

'Time I was off, madam. Morning.'

My caller was Edward Smith. He had just been rung by John Watson. The spare keys of Ferry had been found in Harry's hip pocket and were now due to be returned to

John Watson's office on Monday. 'You'll appreciate that I cannot discuss the cause of this slight delay.'

I nodded to myself. George Ames was one of his clients. 'Of course. But as you may not know this –' and I told him what I had learned from Sandra Black yesterday and about Christine having nursed Ginny Mercer and being Duncan's first soprano and Harry's girlfriend.

'In point of fact I heard all this from Charlotte after Maria Gillon rang her just before I left home. But reliable confirmation is always useful. Maria said the concert's on . . . You had that from Duncan, too? . . . Admirable, we thought. However, to return to your affairs, I have an additional matter for your consideration. Last night by hand delivery to his house John Watson had a firm offer for Ferry Cottage as it now stands from one of his clients who presently wishes to remain anonymous. He is writing to me this morning and very properly did not mention the figure over the phone but did say he considered it a very fair offer. An interesting development, I thought.'

I was not clear what I thought. 'Yes, but stall, please. I need time to think this over.'

'Very prudent. It's the precipitate decisions that keep us in business. Leave it with us – and before I leave you – Charlotte very much hopes Dr Lofthouse is well enough for you both to join us for drinks in tonight's interval.'

I glanced back at the window. Walt had stopped the Land Rover and got out to talk to David. I decided one should not lightly demolish others' hopes and said that would be great.

'Splendid. See you then!'

I swung my chair round for a longer look at the two men in the drive. They stood facing the sea wall and

Jody, on the lead, sat between them. Marlene was vacuuming the carpet in the short arm of the corridor and, I sensed, pining to hear what I thought and tell me what the village was saying about the pile-up, but I was not ready to say anything for public consumption. I switched on the typewriter and got on with today's business post. I had answered three letters when I heard the Land Rover re-starting and saw Murdo had joined David. They were walking back to the house. Murdo always walked slowly, but David no longer walked like an old man. I went on with the letters and had dealt with five more when I heard David coming in through the side door from the hall and telling Marlene that Murdo had hijacked Jody.

I called, 'Got a minute, David? Scientific term in a letter I don't understand.'

'Sure.' He came in quickly, closing the door. 'What's the problem?'

I spread my hands. 'Take your pick, chum. Here's another. Edward's had an anonymous offer for Ferry.'

'Where's the problem?' He sat in the chair Walt had used and took off and polished his glasses. Oddly, for once he looked older without them. 'Only needs lolly to turn it into a very des. little res. in a green belt within easy reach of the sea. And Walt's just said, "Nice little windfall for madam." '

'He told me.' I hesitated. 'And was so chuffed he couldn't hide his relief.'

He half-smiled and replaced his glasses. 'This'll teach me to tell Grandad he's wriggled off the hook again.'

'You've been up to the second landing?'

'Just now to chat with Daph. She hailed me back to the

living as I came through the hall. Long time since my last, so I had another look at your ancestors.'

'Laying or raising ghosts?'

'Neither. Too preoccupied with the living for ghost-busting.' He lit a cigarette and examined the lighted end as if he had it under a microscope. 'After Harry's check yesterday morning, that van was in George's forecourt in view of his front office till Harry drove it off at six. The Coxden lock-up's tucked between the post office and the Lamb. The post office was closed when Harry unloaded and provided a free floor-show for the Lamb's customers on the benches. No one could've nipped unnoticed under the van while Harry's back was turned.'

I took a long breath. 'Walt thinks it was done outside Ferry?'

He looked at me. 'Correction, love. He thinks that's the only time the job could've been done, but, as he said, though George has the odd business rival and dissatisfied customer, neither of them can name one fool enough to take the chance on being sent down for a long stretch just to spit in George's eye. And George says Harry's a lad that never made an enemy in his life.' He stubbed out his cigarette with unusual force. 'Whatever the cause, that poor lad and the rest have picked up the tab. Walt's one bloody angry bloke this morning and I don't blame him.'

'Nor me. I saw he was seething, though he tried to keep it under cover. My news on Ferry only cheered him briefly. Oh – did he tell you Ginny Mercer always fancied Kevin?' He shook his head and I explained quickly. 'To get back to the van – if it wasn't a genuine mechanical failure the Ames brothers'll get him.' I paused but he stayed silent. 'Why don't you think so?'

'Because they'll be playing out of their league.'

I thought this over and nodded reluctantly. 'They're a tough, shrewd bunch, but this is a dangerous psychopath.'

'Tautologous and unproven, Rose.'

'Don't be so damned pedantic. Just tell me how we prove it before he kills someone else.'

He blinked rapidly and said placidly, 'If I didn't love you so much you'd bloody terrify me. You don't need hard evidence when your mind takes off on a frolic of its own. And since you're now hot on the trail of a multiple murderer, tell me for starters how and why he rubbed out Lady G.'

'I can't, as I'm sure he didn't,' I retorted briskly. 'There were too many people present when she died, her death wasn't accidental: Dr Carmody was satisfied it was genuine heart failure. If he'd had the faintest suspicion it wasn't, he would have insisted on a PM and inquest as he did for Max Jones. His word's good enough for me. Yes, I know –' I waved down his attempted interruption – 'last night I said two of the three old women are now dead, but I was only talking off the top of my head. But when I started thinking things out this morning I realised what I've just said about Maud Gillon's death and remembered how just before she died Maria had kept insisting there was a connection between Max and Ginny's deaths and my telling her that was nonsense.' I shuddered. 'Doesn't look that way to me now. Max died in Duncan's cottage. Ginny drowned roughly sixty yards from hers that she's left to me and someone wants to buy sharpish. Too many coincidences happening and I don't like the smell of them.' Again I paused and he said nothing. 'As you haven't told me to clamp down on that Endel blood, you think like me.'

'No, love. I need facts.' He gestured at the telephone. 'And that. May I borrow your office for a few minutes and make some calls?'

I didn't enjoy the faint sound of a trumpet. I jumped up. 'All yours.'

He got up and came round to me. 'It's too bad you won't wed me, Rosie. You're the only woman I've ever met with the nous to act first and ask questions later. As I've told you before. This time round you can have the answers now. I want to make a couple of calls to Maidstone. Time I stood you lunch. I want to book a garden table at the roadhouse just outside that allows dogs and hire a car till Tuesday. Bit far inland, but bigger the town better the chance of getting one at short notice in the tourist season.'

'And of getting one that's unlikely to be recognized locally?'

He smiled. 'Our minds beat as one.'

I didn't smile. 'Not quite. I haven't worked out where you'll hide it at night. Can't be on Endel land. Walt'll have Sam Parker checking it out inside of a couple of hours.'

'He won't tonight if I use your spare garage and lock the doors. Only us and Jody in Endel. Jody's no squealer, and when Murdo reels back to his flat after his customary Saturday-night booze-up, he won't see straight. Anonymity for tonight should be enough.'

My throat had tightened. 'And by more than one sheer coincidence it just so happens that tonight Endel's temporarily childless and everyone who is anyone will be listening to madrigals?'

He took my shoulders in his hands. 'Did I deal the cards?'

'No. David.' I flattened my hands on his chest and looked up into his bruised, quiet face. 'You're just playing the hand you've been dealt. And you're right. Too many jokers in this pack and it's time we took a closer look at one or two. As Duncan's cottage is clean, presumably we start with Ferry. How do we get in without keys? Screwdriver? Chisel?'

'Nail-file should do it. I'll have a penknife on stand by. But this joker's mine. You've got to support Dunk and his mates and leave me convalescing here with Jody. Anyone rings – I've taken her walkies.'

I knew he was right about this and it terrified me for him. 'Promise to keep Jody with you and not leave her in the car?'

'Cross my heart. We all have our own way of getting our kicks, but collecting holes in the head isn't one of mine. Whither I goeth, Jody goeth. After I've cased the joint,' he said as if in afterthought, 'I think I may look up old Norm in Coxden. Come back that way and look out for me and we can finish in convoy.'

I looked at him for more than a few moments. 'You've got this all worked out.'

He shook his head. 'Just working to a very rough blueprint that I think is worth testing. I've no evidence to prove it yet, but unless all this is a load of cobblers, there should be some lying around somewhere.'

Jody found it first and before that Saturday ended.

SEVEN

CHRISTINE AND SANDRA WORE BRODERIE ANGLAISE blouses and long black nylon skirts: Duncan, Stephen and Frank Cross, white shirts, black bow-ties, cummerbunds and evening-dress trousers. The black and white outfits struck exactly the right note for the audience packing the smaller of the two Assembly Rooms in Cliffhill's eighteenth-century town hall from the unusually enthusiastic applause that greeted the singers' arrival on the little stage. Then Duncan, in the middle, stepped forward and his brief, explanatory apology for the changes to the published programme evoked a similar response. And as he waited in the spotlight, his hair a white spun-glass halo, I was near enough to see the relief in his smile.

'Ladies and gentlemen, thank you from the bottom of our hearts. We will begin with John Benet's "All creatures Now Are Merry-minded".'

The large man who had been shown to the empty seat on my right as the lights were going down, folded his arms and settled himself as if for a nap. His ubiquitous British over-forty male holidaymaker's blazer and open shirt made me wonder why it had taken David today to make me recognize belatedly how right he had been about Duncan knowing his public. He knew that with the rare exceptions of the genuinely musical, his indigenous audience regarded this as a social event and the predominantly middle-aged and elderly visitors as a means of spending the long, light evenings off their feet; and that the latter categories shared the common British preference for taking culture in limited doses with an ample break for light refreshments, and disliked hurrying their high teas or early suppers. So the concert started at 8.30, had a twenty-minute interval and ended at ten.

I had booked two third-row stalls on the immediate right of the middle aisle and kept the aisle seat when I asked the plump, dyed blonde in the booking office if she could use my spare ticket.

She accepted it jubilantly. 'Can I not, miss! Keep getting asked for cancellations and I got the five waiting in hope. Never known nothing like it for what you might call a serious group.' She refunded the money. 'But that nice piece about Mr Morgan in tonight's evening paper's fetching 'em in. You seen it, miss? . . . Oh, you should! Bring tears to your eyes!'

From my conversations with friends in the foyer and then in the long, narrow inner hall with a bar at one end and coffee-counter at the other off which lay both Assembly Rooms, the *Cliffhill Evening Argus* had had more than a little help from Duncan and Maria. Again and again; 'Actually, Rose, this weather's so perfect for gardening . . . for tennis . . . for croquet . . . for bowls . . . We had intended giving this a miss. But after Duncan

rang . . . after Maria rang – just had to make the effort.
You on your own? . . . Oh, yes, far more sensible to have
another early night after that shocking attack. Quite
appalling! And the police haven't found him yet . . . oh
dear . . .'

The Gillons were in the front row of my block. Maria,
her hair in a French knot, jet earrings dangling and
purple silk sleeveless shift shimmering, graciously
acknowledged lesser members of the Cliffhill Floral
Society and called to me over heads, 'Poor David too
chewed stringy to face it? Poor sweet! Join us a moment,
darling!' And when I did, 'Is it true the old bat's left you
Ferry? . . . Super! It'll stop giving me the creeps! Yes – I
know, Henry – long chat later, darling!'

I was relieved when the lights went down. Duncan's
opening announcement was the last I heard of the first
half. My body was in my seat; my mind was in a newish
black Rover 2000 until the lights came back on and my
neighbour turned to me courteously. 'Pardon the intru-
sion, miss.' He had a gravelly London voice. 'But from
what the young lady out front said I have reason to
believe I owe you my chance of getting this seat. I'd like
to thank you. Very nice singing.'

I smiled politely and mentally noted his heavy, lived-in
face, hard little eyes and semi-military greying haircut.
'I'm glad you could use it and are enjoying it.'

'Very much.' He tapped his programme. 'It says here,
all amateurs. They must put in a lot of practice to sing so
nicely.'

'I've heard they do. Excuse me –' I exchanged smiles
with the Smiths filing slowly up the queue in the right
aisle, and with Julian, who was down in the queue
coming up the middle. 'Meeting friends.'

'Mustn't keep you, miss.' He half-rose then sat back and studied his programme.

Julian paused and edged sideways to let me in. 'Why no David?' he demanded with professional concern.

'He doesn't dig madrigals. I've left him with Jody.'

'Good healthy sign that he's up to digging in his toes.'

I nodded and changed the subject. 'Where are you sitting? I didn't see you earlier.'

'Far left front. I slipped in after the start as Chrissie asked me to hang around backstage till they were on in case Duncan cracked. Apparently he couldn't have been more off-balance all day if Harry had been his son. He's beginning to pick up.'

'Thank God. How about the others?'

'Stable. Like Duncan once he got on stage.'

'He's hooked on making music.'

'And limelight.' He spoke softly and with rare asperity. 'Conducting satisfies his need to be the centre of attention that off-stage makes him over-dramatise equally major and minor traumas. Purely to placate him, I looked in at the General after tea and chatted up the house surgeon. I couldn't chuck the ethical cat among the pigeons by asking to see Harry, but she's a sensible girl and seems to know her stuff even though she looks as if she's been pulled through a bush backwards. She seems reasonably satisfied with his general condition. I'd just left her when I ran into Chrissie – we'd seen each other around in Benedict's – and as she's now minus Harry's transport and was lugging a suitcase with tonight's costume and tomorrow's clean uniform, I gave her a lift here. Duncan's throwing his after-show party at the Blacks, and she's spending the night in their flat. Which reminds me – I've a message for you from Duncan. He says will you please forgive him for forgetting to invite you and David this morning and prove it by coming to the party. Or must you get back to David?'

'I must,' I said, intrigued he thought so too and that Chrissie, whom he had never mentioned to me before, was an old chum. I thought briefly of a prefect in my second year in a girls' grammar. 'Will you explain to Duncan for me?'

'Sure thing.' He sighed piteously. 'I suppose I'll have to hang on for it.'

'No cross, no crown, Julian.'

He realised he had overplayed the martyr and grinned boyishly. 'Mayn't be too much of a drag. If the second half goes well as the first they'll all be in party mood, but it won't be the same without you. Now what else did I have to tell you? Oh, yes – when Chrissie saw from the wings that you were alone she guessed you'd have to back out of the rave and said would I tell you she's off till two tomorrow afternoon and in the morning Steve's borrowing a van – not, alas, from poor old George Ames – and running her and Sandra over to Littlemarsh to shift what remains to be shifted from your latest acquisition.' He lowered his head to smile reproachfully into my eyes. 'Why haven't you told me the Endel estate now has an extension on the mainland? I had to hear it from father at lunch. Biffer Irons had just told him.'

That figured. Since it was no secret and – to Walt – good news, he would have had it round the marsh before the agricultural dinner hour. 'No time,' I said as we emerged into the crowded hall. The Gillons and Charlotte Smith were in a little group against the wall opposite the coffee-counter from which Edward was struggling through three-deep ranks with a tray laden with plastic mugs. 'And not much of an acquisition.' I added on impulse. 'I don't want or need it. I wish she'd left it to Chrissie.'

For a fleeting moment his smile froze. He recovered swiftly. 'Dear little generous Rose! As well Endel's entailed or you'd give it away. You need someone to take care of these things for you.'

I smiled sweetly. 'I have and here he is. Hi, Edward! Want a hand?'

'Ah, Rose! Well met. Please.' He thrust his tray at Julian. 'Be a good chap and take this over to Charlotte and have mine. If Rose has no objections I would like a word with her.'

'None, Edward.'

Julian said quickly. 'Don't keep her too long, old chap. I may be hauled backstage to cope with artistic temperaments – but if so, you'll understand, Rose?'

I understood so much only the thought of Harry controlled my urge to give three loud cheers. 'Of course.'

He hurried off and Edward shepherded me through the crowd to the empty alcove outside the mayor's parlour. He had spoken to John Watson in the car park before coming in and heard that Ferry was due to be cleared tomorrow morning.

'So Julian's just told me,' I said.

He looked amused. 'Did he also enlighten you on the identity of the anonymous would-be buyer?'

'No. John Watson tell you?'

He shook his neat black head and looked round to ensure we were alone. 'But I have gathered from other sources that he is alleged to be a fairly recent incomer with business interests in Cliffhill who wishes to extend his business premises to the flat above the shop he shares with his wife and for the past few months has been looking for a rural cottage within easy reach of this town.' He smiled conspiratorially. 'He is also alleged to have a fine baritone.' My eyes widened. 'I thought this might enhance your interest in the second half.'

And David's blueprint. 'Well, well – but it makes sense. Only five miles from here. Is his business doing well?'

'Allegedly. Ah!' General Wenden had marched into the alcove. 'Evening, Uncle Nigel.'

'Evening, m'dear – Edward. Been looking for you, Rose. Where's young Lofthouse? Still on the sick-list?'

He dined weekly with his great friends, the Hursts, and Edward was a lawyer. 'Walking wounded, General.'

'Hmmm. Bad business. Too much of it about. Comes from scrapping National Service. They would do it. There it is. Drive yourself up, m'dear? If so, may I scrounge a lift for the home run?'

I was surprised and rather touched by the request. He was renowned for never scrounging lifts or anything else from anyone. 'Of course! Great pleasure.'

'Many thanks, gal. My night vision's not what it was so I leave the night driving to my man. He dropped me here before taking his missus and my car in to some shindig in Astead as this is his night off. But are you sure this won't interfere with your plans?'

I hoped he was referring to Duncan's party. Only hoped, as David had spent longer than I had expected on the phone when I lent him my office this morning. 'Positive General. It'll give me another excuse for missing a party I don't want to attend. Will it suit you if we leave directly the show ends.'

He chuckled and stooped to confide: 'Can't be too

soon for me. I believe in supporting local functions and enjoy a decent symphony, but all these fal-lal-las are wasted on me.'

Edward murmured. 'And on me, Uncle.'

He straightened and looked severely down at Edward's head, which just cleared his shoulder. 'Inevitably, m'boy. Excellent woman, m'wife, but tone-deaf as your father. These things run in families. No getting away from it.' He marched off.

'Coffee, or something stronger, Rose?'

'Coffee, please.'

Edward disappeared for our coffee and I pushed through to the little group round Maria and Charlotte. Henry and Julian had vanished and Maria was addressing the others from the chair. '. . . we really should congratulate them on rising so splendidly to the occasion. My husband and I were just saying we've never heard them sing better. Don't you agree, Rose? Oh, do forgive me –' she apologised to no one in particular – 'but I'm sure you all know Rose Endel? . . . You do? . . . Super!'

Charlotte Smith, a chronically untidy, buxom, redhead who took life – and Maria – seriously, nudged me aside to explain Julian's absence. 'Some crisis backstage.'

I nodded understandingly, apologised for David's absence and asked after her seven-year-old twin sons. But Maria swept between us. 'Darling, I've just had the most super idea!' she announced as Edward rejoined us. 'Henry must buy Ferry from you! I can't imagine you'll want to hold on to it as it's miles from Endel and anyway you're loaded with property and it actually adjoins ours.' She was too excited to notice the glance I exchanged with Edward. 'And if Henry has it I can make certain he never rents it to anyone who gives me the creeps. And do you know –' she played her ace – 'it's still doing that even though it's empty. I'm sure that miserable old biddy is haunting it.'

Charlotte looked perturbed, Edward noncommittal and I hoped my laugh sounded natural. 'I wouldn't bet on that, Maria, but if you're serious, ask Henry to write to Edward. More than that right now, I can't say. Right, Edward?'

'Indeed.' He caught Charlotte's eye and she launched into a long spiel about their twins until the bell rang.

Not having heard the first half I couldn't compare it with the second, but listening properly to the well-timed, intermingling voices, I realised that I had never heard them sing so well. Probably because they sensed their unusually responsive audience, they had all relaxed visibly. While singing, the others watched Duncan. As ever, he was conducting and singing with his back to the audience, but in the pauses for applause after each set of three madrigals, when Duncan spun round, bowing and beaming, the Blacks exchanged private smiles. Frank Cross grinned euphorically at the audience in general and Chrissie's dimpled smile was directed in particular at the far left front row. And from the fixed set of the back of Julian's head, she was on target.

And David that the answer was in Ferry? I glanced at my watch. Only another fifteen minutes and please God, he was now having a drink with the Chief Constable. He only attended official concerts and Lady Hurst was sitting with her great friend, my Mr Smith's widow, in the front row far right. Then the opening of Orlando Gibbons's 'The Silver Swan' diverted my thoughts, and when it ended, stopped the show. The audience insisted on three encores; in every repetition I heard the nightingales and saw the white barn owl clamping a struggling fieldmouse in its beak and the words that had flashed on in my mind like a neon sign.

The final set ended with John Ward's 'Retire my Troubled Soul'. And as I listened to the words set to the sweet, melancholy melody, Ginny Mercer's face rose to the forefront of my mind.

'See life is but a dream whose best contenting
Begun with hope, pursued with doubt.
Enjoyed with fear,
Ends in repenting.'

No repentance in that face. No forgiveness. No quarter, I thought, consciously suppressing a shiver.

It was nearly twenty-past ten when the audience began filing out and my neighbour again addressed me. 'I'd like to thank you again for a very pleasant evening, miss – beg pardon – madam.'

I smiled. 'Not at all. Yes, very pleasant. I hope you enjoy the rest of your holiday. Goodnight.'

'Kind of you to say so, madam. Goodnight.' He followed me into the aisle and as we had both been indoctrinated with the same English tribal customs, we then ignored each other.

I waved to General Wenden standing in his upturned seat a few rows back and as he bowed in response he shot a glance high over my head. He waited till I was parallel with his row then nodded briefly at the large man pausing for him. When we reached the hall the latter moved on ahead. His walk was as unmistakeable as his terminology. I remarked upon this. 'I'll bet he's a cop on hols, General.'

'Got the right feet and right weather for it, m'dear. Where's your car? Corporation park? Sensible gal.'

The town hall stood half-way along the only straight stretch of the narrow cobbled high street. At the southern end this wound sharply downhill; at the northern it was guarded by an old square Norman watchtower that had been built on a cliff lapped by the sea and was now lapped by the Ditch and miles of marsh. The Ditch road was our quickest route to Midstreet, but once we were in my car General Wenden accepted my suggestion that we take the inland road to Coxden Bridge, with a sympathetic nod. 'Passing a recent accident spot used to upset m'wife. Drive miles to avoid it. You please yourself, Rose.' He unfolded his long legs, clipped his safety-belt and took out his pipe and tobacco pouch. 'May I?'

'Please, do. I love the smell of a pipe.'

'So did m'wife.'

It was not long after lighting-up time and the narrow, winding streets of the ancient little town were thronged with strolling visitors ignoring traffic and pedestrian crossings.

'Asking to be winged,' he mused. 'If I were behind your wheel I'd bag a brace. Tiresome things, cataracts. Street lights blind me. Be glad to get out of their range.'

There were no street lights on the country road that ran up and down the low wooded hills that marked the Sussex–Kent border. The lights were on in Wedden village when we ran along the top of Wedden Hill, then the growing darkness returned as the road wound downhill on to Littlemarsh and then Coxden. There was no other traffic or parked cars on Littlemarsh and the shadowy old cottage on its little mound looked as if it had been deserted for centuries – which was more than enough for Maria, and others, to decide it was haunted.

General Wenden turned his head towards it and spoke for the first time since Cliffhill. 'Rum woman, Ginny Mercer. A very fetching little piece in her time, I'm told. Went to seed early. They tell me she's left you old Ferry.'

I guessed 'they' in this context was his old batman, who, with his wife, looked after his bungalow whilst he dealt with his large garden with occasional help from Murdo when short of drinking money. After he and the batman retired to Shepland, General Wenden's home village several years ago, the batman had married a widowed cousin of Mrs Walt. I said, 'Yes. I don't know why.'

'Hmmm. Took to your father, as I recall. Likeable chap, Rosser, with a good head on his shoulders. Like father like daughter,' he said as if that settled the matter. 'What are you going to do with it?'

'I honestly don't know yet.'

He grunted in answer and carefully knocked out his pipe in his dashboard ashtray.

St Mary's, Coxden, struck a quarter-past eleven as I drew up at the STOP sign at the entrance to the main street at the bridge end. The Lamb lay directly opposite across the wide street. All its front lights were off and the nearest of the sparse street lights was too far away to illuminate more than the outlines of the three cars parked in the pub's forecourt. Two were small, pale saloons, the third was larger and black, and all seemed empty. I checked the driving-mirror, reached for the box of tissues in my dashboard shelf and flicked it on to the floor. 'Sorry, need a hankie.' I switched on the inside light, retrieved the box and pulled out a tissue before twitching off the light and driving on. The sudden narrowing of the road and overhanging houses blocked out the sky until we were over the bridge and the wide starlit sky opened out overhead. The moon was not yet up and the stars transformed the marsh to a great black velvet, ruched quilt, the sheep to small, grey, land-based clouds, the dyke rushes to delicate charcoal feathers and the water to black oil. There was very little traffic: the pubs had closed, Saturday-night parties were still on, and in a rural area where most breadwinners worked on the land and the farmers were paying double-overtime on Sundays, even on Saturdays the locals went to bed early. We were about three miles from Coxden when a car coming up behind signalled it was about to overtake and in the driving mirror I glimpsed the long, thin metal grin of the radiator grille of a Rover 2000. When it drew in roughly thirty yards ahead I flashed my lights in appreciation of the driver's signal and breathed out carefully.

My passenger's night vision was better than I had assumed. 'M'youngest boy in Hong Kong's got a 2000. Cost him a fortune shipping it out. Worth it, he says,' he remarked casually, then relapsed into his former silence for the next ten miles. We were still following the Rover when he roused himself. 'Good man, George Ames. Sound mechanic. Not like him to miss a fault.'

I glanced sideways. He was facing the windscreen as if it were a firing squad. 'That's what I think.'

'Hmmm. What's Walt Ames got to say about it?'

'Very little. But I'm pretty sure he doesn't believe the van's brakes were faulty when it left George's garage.'

'He's a good man. Good marsh stock, the Ameses. Hard not to jump the gun in their favour. Particularly for

you. Ameses have worked for Endels for generations. But
– umm – always best to keep your powder dry and
options open, m'dear.'

My instincts vibrated almost audibly. The only previous advice he had ever offered me was on the treatment
of black spot in roses. 'Thanks for the advice, General,
I'll take it.'

'I've found it useful.' Again he fell silent until several
miles on I slowed to take the side turning to Shepland.
'This is where we lose our advance escort party.'

The need to concentrate on the turn into a narrower,
less built-up road with an unfenced cross-dyke on our
left prevented me having to answer or glance at the
vanishing rear lights of the Rover 2000. Neither of us
spoke again until I drew up at his front gate. His
darkened bungalow stood about twenty yards back from
the lane on the inner side of Shepland; his nearest
neighbours' houses were a third of an acre away on either
side and their lights were on behind drawn bedroom
curtains.

'Many thanks, Rose.' He opened his door, swivelled
round with his knees under his chin and lowered his legs
to the ground. 'Don't shift.' He ducked out. 'Off you go!'

'General, please –' I unclipped my belt, slid into his
seat and held open his door. 'Your bungalow's been
empty for hours and – er – I – er – would –'

'Like to see me safely back in barracks, eh?' He
laughed outright. 'By God, it's a long time since a pretty
little filly was concerned for my welfare. Kind thought,
m'dear – but if there's a chap skulking behind my front
door, save your concern for him. An old commando
doesn't forget old tricks. But if it'll ease your mind –
stand-by till I give the all-clear and as a quid pro quo give

me a ring when you're back in Endel. I'll be up.' He saluted smartly, marched off, and after unlocking his front door, kicked it open and switched on the hall light before going in, leaving the door open. Three seconds later he reappeared. 'All clear! Thanks, m'dear. 'Night!'

I drove on, wishing more passionately than at any time since my mid-teens that my father was alive. I was sure I would have liked him as I so liked his friends, and if he had lived to their present age, he would now own Endel and be able to tell me what really lay behind General Wenden's request for this lift back, his warning, and anxiety to hear that I got home safely. I comforted myself with the reminder that David and Jody must now be in Endel, and for the first time since we parted after an early supper in Cranbrook, the tension that had gripped my shoulders began to relax.

It had vanished when I reached the coast road – then clamped on like a vice immediately I turned off by End Cottage. It was in darkness, but Endel blazed with light. All the outside lights and what seemed every ground-floor light in the house was on. Directly I was through the gates I saw the black car parked openly by the front steps and, as I speeded up the drive, David standing by the mounting-block with Jody on a short lead. The lights whitened David's hair and paled the grey of his good suit. He flattened a hand above his glasses to protect his eyes from my headlights, but didn't wave. Still more ominously Jody, instead of barking and leaping joyously, stood four-square, her hackles up, head and tail down, and mute. As I drew up by them David dropped a hand on her head and called quietly, 'Stay put right now, Rose. Let Jody in. She needs you.' His hand came through my window and gripped my shoulder. 'She's had an ugly shock,' he went on in the same quiet, unemotional tone, 'and I'm sorry, love, but I've got to hand you one. Murdo's dead. It looks as if he pitched down the stairs from his flat and hit his head on the flags. She found him first.' I stared numbly at his shadowy face. 'I know, Rosie. I know.' Gently he patted my right cheek. 'Take five. I've rung for Sam Parker and an ambulance.' He reached in, unlocked and opened the nearside back door. 'In you go, Jody. She's home safe.'

Jody leapt on to the front passenger seat and flung the upper half of her trembling body across my lap. I cradled her in my arms, buried my face in her upraised hackles and felt them subside before I raised my head. David was stooped at my open window and our faces were level. 'David. Did he slip?'

He hesitated just long enough to convince me that this time my instincts were right. 'That's the way it looks,' he said. He straightened. 'Here's Parker.'

EIGHT

'I HAVE HERE THE CONTENTS OF THE DECEASED'S pockets that I removed in the presence of Mr Lofthouse and Mr Ames and will leave in your safe-keeping until such time as person or persons unknown with legal claim to these possessions have come forward.' PC Parker spoke in his witness-box voice as he emptied on my desk the first of two small plastic bags. 'Seeing as you were the deceased's employer and landlord, madam.'

I nodded since, as so often in the past hour, I didn't trust my voice.

The ambulance and Dr Carmody had come and gone. Parker, David and Walt – who had arrived unsummoned a few minutes after the doctor, alerted by a phone call from his wife in Shepland – had just returned from unsuccessfully searching Murdo's flat for anything that might help trace his next of kin in Scotland. And I had settled Jody on her mat in the kitchen and belatedly rung General Wenden. I hadn't had to explain the delay. General Wenden, like Mrs Walt, had already heard from neighbours that Parker had been called to Endel because Murdo had had a fatal accident.

'Very sorry to hear it, m'dear. Surly old chap but an old soldier and the only chap I'd trust with my roses. I take it he reported back drunk and disorderly once too often, eh? . . . Bill Carmody said dead between two and three hours when he examined his body shortly after midnight? Why was he back well before closing time eh? . . . You've no idea? Hmm. No sign of foul play? . . . Hmmm . . .'

Parker laid in a neat row an old, closed penknife; a small screwdriver and pair of pliers; a battered gunmetal pocket-watch, still working despite its smashed glass, that showed five past one; four little bundles of old string; a greyish, oil-smeared handkerchief; an unopened packet of twenty Marlboro; a squashed empty packet of ten Kensitas and a ringed bunch of keys on a long, thin, tarnished metal chain. 'Am I correcly informed these are keys to your property, madam?'

'Yes, Mr Parker.' I exchanged glances with Walt, who was sitting on David's left across the desk. Neither of their expressions gave anything away, but Walt's face seemed to have aged years in hours. Paradoxically, David's looked younger and I sensed the seething anger beneath his stolid front. I identified the keys. 'This Yale – his flat's front door. This one and this mortice – the rat-poison cupboard in the spare garage. The other mortice – his yard door – my garage – the spare garage – and the back door of this house.'

'I see.' Parker brushed one end of the thin black moustache above his thin lips, unhooked the keys and laid them on my blotter then added more notes in his open notebook. He was on David's right with his chair adjusted to face both sides of the desk, and he now sat back and gave us another cold, comprehensive glance before taking from the second bag an old brown plastic wallet and a clinking envelope. He emptied the last and while he flicked into line one shilling, three sixpences and five pennies, David caught my eye. 'Upon removing the wallet and loose change,' intoned Parker, 'I requested both witnesses to check with me the wallet's contents and sum of money in notes and loose change.' He handed me the wallet. 'You will find herein one driving licence in the deceased's name, six old betting slips and twenty used one pound notes. Be so good as to count the notes, madam.'

David's warning controlled my reaction. I needed the help. Murdo had never left a pub until he ran out of cash. 'Twenty, Mr Parker. In all, £20 2s 11d.'

'I'll make out a receipt that will require your signature on both copies, madam.'

He only took about a minute. It took me much less to recognise clearly what lay behind David's warning and earlier suggestion that Parker might find some useful old letters or photos in Murdo's flat. David had been one of the very few visitors Murdo had ever had. I hadn't been in his flat since it was last repainted three years ago. Murdo had jealously guarded his domestic privacy and on the rare occasions when he had a guest, it had always been someone he liked. But though he had liked Daph and Marlene, he had flatly refused my suggestion that they help with his cleaning. 'I've aye fended for ma'self, ma'am. I've nae wish to change ma ways . . .' Nor had I ever known him do so – until tonight.

'Just sign here, please, madam – ta.' Parker put away

his receipt book and shook his near crewcut dark head at David's offered cigarettes.

'Ta, Mr Lofthouse.' Walt accepted his first cigarette in my office. 'Left mine by me telly.'

'No problem, Mr Ames. I'm loaded. Help yourself.' David placed his Senior Service and lighter on the desk between them.

Parker's beaky nose twitched disapprovingly. He was tallish, spare, in his mid-thirties, a non-smoker, was never known to drink more than a half of shandy and was reputed to have smiled on his wedding day. His intelligent humourless face wore the habitual expression of a man who had seen it all and hadn't liked any of it. 'Would you know if the deceased was in the habit of coming back early on a Saturday night, madam?'

'No, Mr Parker. But I didn't keep tabs on him. He may have done so occasionally.'

Walt protested mildly, 'You know his habits better than most, Sam, seeing you're always outside the Crown closing time on Saturday nights. Mind you – from what he was putting back sevenish when I dropped in for my pint, I shouldn't wonder if he finished off his pay packet sharpish and stepped back for what he got stashed away from odd-jobbing and striking lucky on a horse for the once.'

'That's as may be, Walt. But if you ask me, he struck lucky on more than the one horse from the number of empty half-bottles we found up his flat along of the empty whole Mr Lofthouse identified as one of the two he fetched back with him.'

I looked down at the keys on the desk. David had often tipped Murdo cash and cigarettes, but never whisky. When we left for Maidstone on what was now yesterday morning, both of David's bottles had been on the sideboard in the dining room. By then Marlene and Daph had gone, Murdo had still been working in the kitchen garden and Endel had been empty until David got back tonight. And the only spare set of keys to my flat should still be locked in this desk.

'All right to put these keys away, Mr Parker?'

'Your property, madam.'

'Right.' I unlocked my key drawer. My flat keys were there. I dropped in Murdo's, relocked the drawer and glanced at David. He had his cigarette back under a microscope and Walt ground rather than stubbed out his.

He said, 'Seeing Mr Lofthouse been back over the week I reckon his bottle been empty nigh as long. Mind you – like the Old Doctor said, from the smell of whisky still on him after lying out the two to three hours, he'd had more than a skinful tonight, and seeing his stairs is steep and narrow, no surprise to him an old chap Murdo's age took a tumble.'

No surprise to the doctor, General Wenden, or anyone who knew Murdo. No signs of foul play. Same pattern. Maria, I thought icily, should take a bow.

Before Dr Carmody left he drew me aside. 'I'm exceedingly sorry about this, Rose,' he said, 'but from the scuffs on the top stairs, the marks on the flags and his posture, I've little doubt that he slipped, pitched down backwards and as his cap had dropped off and he had left his yard door open, he landed on the back of his unprotected head. The momentum of his fall could well account for the damage to his skull that killed him instantly. But as his age and heavy drinking may have caused the coronary or stroke responsible for his fall, I've just told Parker I'm reserving my opinion on the precise cause of death until I get the pathologist's report.'

David switched off the microscope and stubbed the cigarette out. 'As the cash and unopened fags hadn't been lifted, there can't have been any stray tramps round Endel tonight.'

Parker bristled. 'I'd not missed that, Mr Lofthouse. I'll not delay you further, madam.' We all rose and he reached for the police motorcyclist's helmet and guantlets he had left on the nearest filing cabinet. 'I'll keep you informed regarding the inquest. I take it you'll be here for it, Mr Lofthouse?'

'If not, I'll come back for it.'

'I'll inform my superiors, sir.' Parker turned to me. 'And keep you informed of any further developments that may arise, madam.'

'You mean in connection with his next of kin?'

He hesitated deliberately. 'As you say.'

'Thank you, Mr Parker. And for all your help.'

'That's why I'm here. Sorry I was wanted. Not a nice homecoming for you after the concert. Go nicely, did it?'

'Very. Full house.'

'That'll have pleased Mr Morgan.'

David asked, as if he and I were alone, 'How did he handle the tenor, Rose?'

'He was brilliant. They all were.'

Parker stiffened like Jody at a rat-hole. 'I take it you gave it a miss, Mr Lofthouse?'

David smiled slightly. 'Christ, yes. Too arty for me and I wanted to give my hired job another run.'

'Oh, yes? Going nicely, is she?'

'Very smoothly. She's the first 2000 I've handled, and

140

from what Sir Norman Hurst told me tonight about his wife's they are very smooth jobs.'

I added chattily, 'When you overtook us south of Coxden General Wenden told me one of his sons cherishes his 2000.' I looked at Parker. 'I gave the general a lift from the concert as his man's got his car tonight.'

He was a quick learner. 'Very nice for the old gentleman I'm sure, madam,' he said, pleasantly for him. 'Time I was off. 'Night, all.'

'I'll see you out, Mr Parker, and put away the cars.' David held out a hand for the keys. 'May I use your spare garage, Rose?'

'Sure.' I gave him my car keys, unlocked the drawer and handed him Murdo's. 'Thanks again, Mr Parker. Goodnight.'

David had made it so obvious that he wanted to talk privately to Parker that Walt made no attempt to leave. He stood by his chair, steady as the rock he had become in my life, and I felt as if my feet had suddenly sunk in quicksand.

'Walt, can you use a drink? I can and so will Mr Lofthouse when he comes back.'

'I'd not say no to just the one, ta, madam.'

'Fine.' I gestured at the pathetic little collection on the desk. 'I'll just shove these in the safe, first.'

'I can do that for you, madam. I got my safe keys on me.' He hesitated. 'Would you mind if I give my wife a tinkle? Her brother-in-law'll have fetched her home in his sidecar, but young Kevin's up Astead with his mates for the night and she'll be alone, and fretting, I shouldn't wonder.'

'Do ring her first. And thanks for dealing with this lot. I'll be a few minutes. Jody'll need a bit of time.'

He opened the door for me and I heard him dialling as I went into the kitchen. Jody was pathetically pleased to see me. She hadn't touched the large marrowbone I had left with her for comfort, but she began licking it when I got off her mat and washed my hands before taking out the icecubes and setting a drinks tray. I took the tray to the dining room but didn't switch on the light. After Dr Carmody left, David and Walt had switched off the lights in all the unoccupied ground-floor rooms, but as the outside lights were still on and the curtains open there was enough light to see the single bottle of whisky on the sideboard. I put the tray on the table, dried my palms on my skirt and moved closer to the locked window.

David and Parker had backed under the light at the front east corner of the house. Parker was writing in his notebook, and from David's stance I could tell he was dictating. The strip on the back of his head looked like a long dark scar. I squeezed shut my eyes to black out the image of the blood streaming from the gash on Tuesday evening, and it was superimposed by the far more hideous condition of the back of the head of the small, scraggy, grotesquely stiffened figure lying face down in the yard tonight.

'Only minimal bleeding,' Dr Carmody had muttered, sitting back on his heels. 'Wouldn't expect more when the skull's smashed in like an eggshell. Give me a hand turning him, Parker . . .'

I retched involuntarily, backed to the sideboard and needed both my shaking hands to move the whisky and siphon to my tray. I had taken it to the office, given Walt a drink and picked up my own when the revving of the motorbike and my car evoked a ferocious response from

Jody. I called to her and when she quietened said, 'She's very shaken. She loved Murdo, and he, her.'

'Aye. Fondness for dogs, he had. She'll pine. Best not try fetching her back the yard till she's ready. She'll know when.' Walt sat in his former chair cradling the glass in his large, strong hands. My eyes filled with tears and he added gently, 'Same as yourself, madam. You'll miss him.'

'Dreadfully.' I mopped my eyes and my mind flashed back to my first cataclysmic weekend in Endel. 'I've never known Endel without him. We hit it off from my first visit because I had clicked with my cousin's old Labrador, Dolly.'

He nodded sympathetically. 'Nice old bitch was Dolly. Shame she copped it from a falling tile your first gale.'

I looked into my glass. Murdo had known Dolly had not been killed by a falling tile. She had been poisoned by Robert, who had privately told me David had battered her to death. Murdo had been sober when I had coaxed the truth from him and as Walt still accepted Robert's official version of Dolly's death, Murdo, drunk or sober, had kept his mouth shut. But someone hadn't trusted him to do that tonight. 'That upset Murdo badly.'

'I heard.' Walt sipped his drink. 'Your garden'll miss him,' he said, not callously but with the born country-man's acceptance that death was part of life and irrespective of grief must never be allowed to disrupt the tilling of the land and tending of the livestock. 'I best look out for a new gardener, pronto. Turn your back on a garden early June and out of hand before you turn round. I'll fetch one of the lads down from the farm afternoons to keep it in hand till you're suited.'

Being half-marsh controlled my voice, not my thoughts. 'Thanks. Anyone in mind?'

He rubbed his jaw. 'Young Tom Bagley keeps his mum's garden a treat, but he's that cackhanded with machines I'd not trust him with your rotoscythe.'

My mental pattern had grown terrifyingly clear and had only a few remaining gaps. I said vaguely, 'Murdo wouldn't trust anyone but Kevin with it and only he kept it going. But every time I suggested getting a new one he said it was just fine just now.'

'He knew his machines. Mind you, he should, having put in nigh on twenty years as a fitter in Glasgow before he was called up the Gunners and copped the one in his chest Anzio that bought his ticket and had him turning gardening as he had to work out in the open.'

I stared at him momentarily. One less gap. 'I'd forgotten he'd been a fitter.'

Walt nodded and we fell silent, thinking our own troubled thoughts. The cream linen curtains were closed across the open window to deter moths, gnats and maybugs attracted by the office light. The nocturnal croaking chorus of frogs was growing drowsy and the tide ebbing out over the pebbles sung a soft requiem for Murdo.

The Rover had not been moved when only Jody heard David's quiet return. His 'David, Jody!' silenced her. 'Too much clutter in the spare garage. I'll shift it later today,' he said, accepting a drink.

'I can give you a hand with it now, Mr Lofthouse.'

'Thanks, Mr Ames. It can wait. Won't hurt it to stay out for what's left of tonight.' He sat in Parker's chair, offered Walt a cigarette and lit them both. 'Parker doesn't miss much,' he remarked conversationally. 'He's just asked why I'm smoking Senior Service not Marlboro.' He looked at me. 'I told him in Murdo's flat I'd given him one hundred and kept the other. I've just told him outside that mine have gone, and anyway I prefer English. Then he wanted a recap of the little I've ever known of Murdo's provenance. He thinks the Glasgow police may turn up something. I doubt it.' He turned to Walt. 'Glasgow's a big city, the MacDonalds are the biggest clan in Scotland, and as far as I know, Murdo never had form.'

'Kept a clean sheet down here, Mr Lofthouse,' Walt said. He paused reflectively. 'I was stationed outside Glasgow three months, back in the last do. Needle in a haystack be a sight easier to find than folks of an old chap as not been back best side of twenty-five years and never had so much as a Christmas card from his folks, if he had any. I never reckoned he had.'

'Nor did I.' David put his barely touched drink on the desk and our eyes met. 'It would save Parker one hell of a lot of paperwork if he'd been born on the marsh.'

His cue made no sense. I picked it up blindly. 'Yes. He'd only have to get on his bike and take a look round the old graveyards.'

'You're not far wrong, madam. All yours down Midstreet. All mine, St Martin's.'

David smiled. 'You'll be the odd one out when your time comes, Rose. All the other born-Endels: "Born Endel House, 19— 18— 17— 16— something".'

The ghost of a smile touched Walt's eyes. 'Same as me, madam.'

David and I looked at him enquiringly. I asked, 'You weren't born in St Martin's?'

145

He shook his head. 'My old mum was in service up London when she married my dad and had me.'

'I never knew that.'

His face and tone softened as always when talking of his beloved mother. 'Long before your time, seeing as I come last week of 1916 and the two weeks before Mr Rosser. My dad was over in France having gone for a trooper in the Arumchester Yeomanry early 1915. Mind you, he been courting my mum long before the war and she went into service for Mrs Franklin up Astead. MP for Astead was Mr Franklin, and first year of the war he moved his good lady and most the servants up his London house, Kensington.'

I stiffened inwardly and avoided looking at David. 'Wasn't that Mr Franklin Lady Gillon's older brother who died some time in the 1930s?'

'That's right, madam. Gone 1934, the year after his good lady. A real nice lady was Mrs Franklin, my mum used to say. Expected her cards, she had, when my dad got his leaf to marry her March 1916, but Mrs Franklin kept her on and put her on lighter work while she was carrying me. She let her have me in her house and keep me with her till my dad got his demob and fetched us back St Martin's lambing-time 1919. And your grandad, madam, took my dad straight back on his old job as under-shepherd.' He looked from me to David. 'Not many employers did as much for an ex-serviceman them days. No law forcing them to keep the lads' jobs open like after the last do.'

David nodded. 'I've heard my dad on that. Your dad was lucky to have a good guv'nor.'

'Aye. Hard man as wouldn't be crossed, was old Mr Endel, but good guv'nor.' He drained his glass and stood up. 'That went down nicely, ta, madam. Time I got back to my wife. You'll not mind me leaving you to finish your drink, Mr Lofthouse?'

David had risen. He gestured apologetically. 'Taking it slowly; on medication.'

He wasn't. I felt the sand seeping over the tops of my boots. 'I'm sorry you're so late, Walt.'

'Late for us all, madam.'

David held open the door. 'Like me to turn the outside lights off when Mr Ames has left, Rose?'

'Please.'

David left the door open and followed Walt out. I heard them walking along to the front door and then David returning and going into his bedroom. The master switch for the outside lights was on the kitchen wall by the side door to the hall. I didn't hear David going on to the kitchen. I went to the window, opened the curtains and was watching the rear-lights of the Land Rover disappearing down the drive when the outside lights went out. There was no other traffic on the coast road and the silence of the last hour before a fine summer dawn, when even the frogs slept, settled over the marsh. The waning sickle moon was high in the black starry sky, the black silk sea was creeping out over the sand, the sea wall, sandbags and End Cottage were shadows in the shadowy darkness, and the great overhanging roof cast a black shadow over Endel. The shadows in my mind were far blacker.

'Charitable family, Lady G.'s.' David was beside me, dangling his empty airline bag from one hand.

I looked up at him sharply. 'You can't seriously believe –'

'When did I believe anything without proof, love?' He

147

shut the curtains. 'Come and look in this.' He backed to the desk and held open the empty bag. 'When we left for Maidstone, two bottles on the sideboard and an unopened twenty Marlboro in here. I've just told Parker I can prove I didn't give Murdo the whisky and swear on oath I left the fags in this, but I can't prove he didn't nick both and would lay a packet the only fingerprints on that bottle are Murdo's, Parker's and mine – unless you touched it?'

'Can't remember. But Murdo couldn't have nicked them! My only spare flat keys –' I jerked a thumb – 'in that drawer. Only Walt and I have the others and nothing'll persuade me that Walt –'

'Hold it, Rosie! Murdo had a back-door key and when I horsed round turning on lights your side-door bolt was open.'

I gaped. 'I bolted it before we left. I can swear to it.'

He said quietly, 'I'd guessed that. But I didn't see you bolt it and you'd a lot on your mind then that any good lawyer would ferret out and go to town on. And under oath I'd have to say that though I liked Murdo I'd never have trusted him with my wallet or my whisky. Nor would anyone who knew his thirst –' suddenly the anger he had been containing for hours ripped out – 'and that's what bloody killed him! But unless the PM sheds more light, it'll be another death by bloody misadventure. Balls! Somehow – some time yesterday the poor old bloke caught on and the sod knew this and made a date here ostensibly to pay him to keep his mouth shut, then made sure of the job and planted the cash and fags on him to provide the motive for his coming back early and to confuse the issue if foul play's suspected.'

'He's good at confusing –' my own temper reached

flashpoint – 'but caught on to *what*? Obviously you know, so for God's sake tell me. I still don't know what you found in Ferry or got from Sir Norman. Come out of that bloody computer, man, and level with me!'

'Christ, when have I had time to tell you anything? Ferry was a total washout. No sign of a cellar – nothing that I wouldn't have expected to find there, and Harry had shifted enough for me to have a good look round. Old Norm –' he took a long breath and went on more calmly – 'was better value. Consequently, the first thing I've got to tell you is that this is where you say "I bloody told you so." '

I flopped into my desk chair. 'Dope-smuggling.'

'Uh-huh. Wrong merchandise. Even Homer sometimes nods and you are still one very smart cookie. Diamonds.'

'*What*?'

'Uncut diamonds from Holland. Listen, love.' He sat on the edge of the desk and tapped the back of his head. 'After I told old Norm that I went along with your unproven theory on this job he said we might well be right even though the GBH didn't fit the picture given him by his chaps. I asked the obvious and after a heavy silence he said he saw no reason for not assuaging my understandable curiosity. Then he told me that for the past twelve months they've been pretty certain diamonds have been coming in this way in small enough quantities to be passed hand to hand from a fishing boat off the coast to the final delivery point in some back office in Hatton Garden, but they've been unable to lay a finger on anyone. Very smooth, very professional operation, he said. Strictly non-violent and no hint of trouble with the natives who, as one, have seen nowt and heard nowt.'

'Huh,' I snorted. 'So what else is new?'

'My GBH. Norm said owing to the previous lack of violence they initially discounted my coming into the picture until our Sam came up against the same wall of silence. Quote: Made my chaps wonder if it might be worth keeping a discreet eye on our musical friends. Unquote.'

I nodded to myself. 'There was one in your seat tonight.'

He looked at me over his glasses. 'Say again.'

I told him all I had noticed about the large man, what he had said to me, that I thought General Wenden had recognised him and what the general had said to me on the drive back. 'I'm now sure he knows as much, and probably more, about all this than you.'

'Safe bet. Norm's best mate. What else did you pick up at the rave?'

'Amongst much else, that we've missed the one Duncan was throwing in the Blacks' flat after the show.' I told him all I had had from Edward and Julian in the interval and noticed in the second half. 'Julian's too hooked on Christine to hide it but she may well need lolly to keep him hooked – no!' I had to stop. 'I'm getting carried away. Yes, she's a go-getter, but she's too bright and too sensible to play with fire – and that's precisely what playing along with people as unstable as Duncan and Sandra would be. And Harry's too honest to touch anything bent with a bargepole.' David just looked at me. 'OK, so I'm a lousy judge of men. But you like Harry.'

'Oh, aye. Nice lad.' The computer in his eyes was flicking over at top speed and he got off the desk and drifted round the office. 'Yep,' he mused. 'I'm with you on the lovely Chris. Tough and sexy as hell, but straight as Harry. Very handy protective cover for their mates.'

'Until Harry caught on and had to be silenced.'

He faced me. 'You can't guarantee killing anyone in a road accident. People often stagger no worse than shocked out of the most disastrous smashes. But from the timing of Harry's, I've thought since I heard of it that there's a high degree he caught on to something in Ferry. Christ knows what. I bloody missed it.'

I thought aloud. 'Ginny Mercer must have known what it was . . . David! And Steve Black! That's why he's so keen to buy it.'

Suddenly his face closed. 'I wouldn't bet on the last, love.' He turned away and opened the curtains. The first faint streaks of grey had appeared in the eastern sky. He said, with his back to me, 'Our Steve may or may not have been pussy-footing around this joint yesterday, but sure as hell he wasn't supping drams with Murdo in his flat last night. And if the answer is in Ferry, be daylight before we get there.' He spun round. 'Let's hope Chris is too hooked on Jule to see straight. Having the Blacks on hand will protect her back temporarily, not permanently.'

It was then I knew what he dreaded having to tell me. I couldn't bear to voice it either. Not yet. He had hauled me out of quicksand once: now it was my turn to do that job for us both. I looked at his barely touched glass and stood up slowly. 'I'll get into jeans and get Jody. Be easier to read your blueprint in daylight, David.'

NINE

'I DON'T LIKE THIS COTTAGE, DAVID. AND IT DOESN'T like me.'

He sat back on his heels by the hearth. 'Time was when you felt that about Endel.'

'That was only in my first weekend when I was too thick to recognise that what was wrong with the atmosphere came from Robert and June, not the house. I noticed the difference first time I went back into the ruins with Mr Smith and the insurance assessor the day after their funeral.' I looked round the half-emptied little living room that was cluttered with empty teachests. We had left it to last, as there were no cupboards in the old, unfaced brick walls or mats on the bare wooden floor. 'Ginny's was eight days back, but I'm smelling what I first smelt in Endel far more strongly than the rising damp and dry rot.' I shivered. 'Maria's right. Ginny's still haunting this.' I hesitated. 'Think that's why she left it to me?'

'You've always said she had all her marbles.' He lay on

his face to look up the chimney. 'Nowt but charred brickwork, soot and a nest up top.'

'Jackdaws,' I said absently. My mind was fixed on the final black patch in the pattern. I had known old Mrs Ames well. She had loved all her sons, and especially Walt, her favourite.

David sat up and cleaned his glasses. 'When do jackdaws start breeding?'

'Oh – mid-April.' I stared into the wide, open hearth that was speckled with the soot and bits of twig that had come down the chimney since it was last swept. 'They like nesting in old chimneys and she won't have needed a fire in here for the last couple of months.' I looked at his tired, unshaven face, then did another survey as if playing pelmanisim. The early sunshine slanting through the two low front windows was beginning to warm the room. But not me. Cold stuff, quicksand. I kicked aside the near-empty old log basket and sat by him on the floor. 'We've missed something.'

'As we've toothcombed the joint and found Sweet Fanny bloody Adams, you tell me what.' He sounded as despairing as I felt. 'Make it snappy. We'll have to make tracks soon. Farms'll be waking.'

'And old Nora. She's always up by five. Like old Ginny.'

'How do you know that?'

'Oh – er –' the sand was seeping into my mind. 'Forgotten . . . no! Yes, she told me the time she told me she stored apples six months.' I mimicked the harsh, broad-vowelled old voice. ' "Summer or winter can't abide my bed after five of a morning." ' And in my own voice: 'We still haven't found where she kept them. But as the kitchen's cold enough, I could be wrong about that too.'

'Join the queue, Rosie.'

I shook my head helplessly. Jody sensed our need for comfort and left the open doorway to the living room to squeeze between us. The change of scene had been good therapy for her grief, but she was now as tense as when we left the Rover up against the marsh-side hedge of Potts House and walked back here. She sat upright, her ears cocked for sounds only she could hear, and eyed the empty hearth as if it were burning spitting logs.

The birds were still singing the dawn chorus, the light was returning fast and the eastern horizon was rimmed with pinkish gold. We walked quietly, not talking. We hadn't talked much on the drive up: our mental communication was too close to need spoken words and neither of us was a masochist. I held Jody's lead and she kept brushing against me, looking up at us warily, too perturbed by our mood to do more than glance perfunctorily at the sleeping sheep, rustling moorhens and even the rabbits streaking for cover as they scented her. But when we stopped to examine the grass verge that had been flattened by tractor treads, she began snuffling the ground, picking up remembered and new scents.

David said, 'Handy things tractors and so much part of this scene that no one notices them.'

I nodded, and we looked up and down the empty road, at the lightless, sleeping village on the inner end of Wedden Hill, at the closed curtains of all the back windows of Potts and the three small uncurtained windows at the front of Ferry. I said, 'Looks empty, but if not Jody'll tell us. She won't bark. She never does on other people's property, but she'll tell us quietly.'

'She was dead quiet last evening.' He stroked her head. 'This is where you and I came in, mate.'

We crossed the wooden bridge and knew from Jody's lack of interest in the locked front door that there was no one behind it before we peered through the windows. 'Tight fit for you, David.'

'And too public. Kitchen's the best bet. It's a bit bigger, the only one at the back and only visible from Lady G.'s rear windows. No sign of life at any of them yesterday.'

'The telly's on in the drawing room at the front.'

'God's gift to burglars. Let's get round.'

The tiny, rotting-fenced back garden was sheltered on the left by the far hedge of the back garden of Potts and backed by another cross-dyke and the gently rising foot of a low, empty, green hill. The vegetable patch had been massacred by the rabbits in the last twelve days and young weeds were coming up between the neat rows of marigolds and sweet williams in the flowerbed just outside the kitchen window, a few feet left of the back door. A narrow cinder track ran up the right side of the garden to a battered brick privy with a weather-pitted wooden door hanging open, and in the opposite far corner half hidden by massive clumps of partially flattened nettles, was the old disused wellhead that on Friday morning Edward told me had been boarded down when mains water was connected in the 1950s. David said he had tested the boards last night. 'I couldn't shift 'em. Jody went to town on 'em. Rodents below. Let her go and she'll tell you.'

There were no sheep this side of the road, so I unhooked the lead. Jody ignored the privy, streaked through the nettles and snuffled and scratched the well cover. 'All I need,' I said.

He patted my shoulder. 'Relax, love. She didn't smell any within, probably because most of the ground floor's cement.' He took off his jacket, handed it to me and opened his penknife. It took him under a minute to open the smallish, single-paned low window, but much longer to squeeze through, red-faced and blaspheming. Jody leapt and I slid in, in seconds. Jody righted herself, looked about alertly, then raced into the living room through the open door at the front of the uncarpeted wooden stairs running up the inner wall like a boxed-in ladder to the open bedroom door. She was back and up the stairs before I had taken in more than the similarity to the interior of End Cottage, which had no cellar. The narrow kitchen ran the length of the back wall and backed against it was an old stone sink, a small, elderly Calor gas cooker, and an Edwardian hand-mangle. The sink had the only tap in the cottage and beneath it was an old tin hip-bath. From the marks on the back wall, Harry had shifted out a small dresser before or after he cleared the two rows of hooks and the minute larder to the right of the living-room door. The cement floor was strewn with sawdust and three empty teachests were backed against two smaller doors just under and beyond the top of the stairs.

'Broom and log cupboards, David?'

'Yes.' He put his jacket on the draining-board and loosened his tie. He hadn't changed out of his suit, to save time. 'Harry didn't get round to them but – no dice.' He shifted the chests and opened the first door. 'Both brick-sided and roofed, cement-floored and solid as hell.'

I crawled round his legs, pushed aside old broom

handles, gardening tools, oil lamps, jam jars of candle ends, a half-empty can of paraffin and ran my fingers round the floor edges. 'Not even a mousehole.' I looked up. 'Same size as the one in End.'

'I never measured it. This is four foot by four, and five high.'

I sniffed. 'She didn't keep apples in here.'

'Nor here. It's deeper.' He opened the second door and two new logs rolled out over the top of the five bayboards holding the pile in place. The removable boards were slotted into sturdy wooden struts embedded in concrete on either side, just inside the door. Jody pounced on a log.

'Drop that, Jody! Splinters are bad for your guts!' I threw it back, David chucked in the other and we backed to let in more light. The bayboards jammed the logs against the sides and back wall to within a foot of the uneven rough brick roof. 'To be precise, ten inches. This one's four by five two, and five high.' David on his knees fed a thin, metal expanding tape measure in beneath the bottom bayboard, forced it under the pile, slightly twisted it and the edge grated on cement. 'Yep. Five two. Roof matches. Discrepancy tell you anything?'

'Damn all. Every recessed cupboard in Endel's a different size.' I looked up and down the inner wall and kitchen floor. 'If this had a cellar, steps down should have been around here.'

'Maybe she cemented them over.'

'Oh, no. A city-bred incomer might. Not a country-woman. Cellars are too useful, especially in a joint this small.'

'Oh, aye.' He was about to stand up when he looked more closely at the floor and ran his hands over it.

'Rough, amateur job and newer than I thought last night.'

'How new?'

'I'd say a year or two.' He looked up at me. 'Could she have done the job?'

I thought a moment of more than the weight of wet cement. 'She may have had a little help from her friends, but even if not, probably. She was agile and tough. This time last year she was up a ladder outside mending her roof.'

'Where did she get the ladder? There isn't one inside or out.'

'No idea. Never asked. Borrowed it, I expect.' I sniffed the kitchen air that even after the long hot spell was damp and chilly. 'She could have stored apples in here or the larder. She didn't. There's not even a hint of the cidery scent that lingers ages after an apple store's emptied.'

He stood up dusting his hands and shutting the log-store.

'Only the loft,' I said.

He shook his head. 'Hasn't been used in years. Come and see.'

The uncleared bedroom was so small that the narrow, single wooden bed took up most of the floor. The bed was backed against the rear wall to face the dormer window, and above it in the low ceiling was a small, hinged trapdoor. He shifted the bed, pushed up the trapdoor, levered himself higher but couldn't get in more than his head. 'Nowt but dust and muck. I'll give you a lift.'

'In a minute. Sun's rising.'

We stood a little back from the closed window whilst the sun rose in a golden haze that gilded the village on Wedden Hill, the soft green hillside, the vivid green of Littlemarsh and turned the dyke water a shining bronze. The dew sparkled on every blade, leaf, petal, the pinkish-white backs of the shorn sheep, the folded black wings of the flocks of strutting magpie, the dark brown wings of the curlew and the metallic green of the lapwing. Two herons, keeping their distance from each other, fished one-leggedly on opposite sides of the main dyke; a kestrel hovered near-stationary just outside the dormer window; a jackdaw cawed directly overhead; and somewhere nearby a barn owl in a hollow tree or secret crevice was settling down to sleep.

I suppressed a shudder and turned back to the room that looked untouched since Ginny Mercer tidied herself before cycling to her last WI meeting in Coxden. Aside from the bed there was only an uncurtained hanging cupboard, a small, woodwormed rosewood chest of drawers that doubled as dressing-table under a plastic-framed mirror hanging on the wall, a three-legged wooden stool and a much-washed rag bedside rug. I said, 'Doesn't look as if Harry got up here.' I looked at the open trap. 'He certainly couldn't have got through that. I can.'

David said nothing until he had lifted me through to my waist. His hold tightened. 'That's your lot. Those rafters'll be slippery as hell under the muck and there's only plasterboard between. We need you crashing through this ceiling like I need another hole in the head.'

I didn't argue. The sunlight shafting through the innumerable cracks in the front of the steeply slanted

roof illuminated the entire loft. The rafters and plaster-
boarding were layered with dust, bird- and mice-drop-
pings and pocked with tracks, and despite the clean air
seeping in there was a sickly smell of decay. 'You're right,
David. No one up here for years.'

He set me down and closed the trap. 'I checked these
walls, floor, the bedding and drawers last evening. Want
to re-check?'

I thought of Murdo's wallet and shook my head.
'Room in the loft, but no big enough hiding-place in here.
He's got to have hidden it somewhere, but not at home –
oh God! Endel's basement's riddled with cellars and
Murdo may've stumbled on to it collecting up dead rats.'
I saw the expression that flickered through David's eyes.
'Not in your blueprint?'

'That on present showing is a right balls-up.' He went
ahead down to the living room.

David blinked at the hearth. 'Won't she have needed a
fire to have a bath in here and dry her washing?'

'Not in the weather we've had for weeks. Logs don't
cost much, but she always gave me the impression she
had to watch every penny – as this joint demonstrates.
Had this been council property it would have been
condemned years ago. But as she seems to have liked it,
I'm glad for her sake it wasn't. If Maria really wants it,
she can't have it too soon for me. And she can bring her
own bell, book and candle.'

He nodded noncommittally and fished one of the few
logs from the basket. 'Old and dry as timber. Last
winter's. New lot in store. Presumably she stocked up in
summer when it's cheaper?'

My mind did a double-take. 'No. I mean yes, they are

cheaper and new – but they shouldn't be –' I jumped up – 'because she didn't!'

His expression quickened. 'Why not?'

'I've just remembered her once telling me she always got hers from Tom Matthews because his were cheapest and he never charged for delivery as his tractors kept passing her door.' He was on his feet rolling up his shirtsleeves. 'Matthews only delivers after he's finished autumn ploughing and hedging-and-ditching – like Walt from our woods. No good farmer wastes his men's time logging in summer. God, am I thick! So obvious, I missed it!'

'You and me both, love. We'll need the extra.' He grabbed a teachest, I grabbed another and Jody bounded after us back to the kitchen.

'Sit, Jody! Guard these!'

She sat on her haunches, her ears up, hackles down, turning her head from side to side as we ducked in and out of the log-store. We had filled one and half-filled a second chest when the removal of the third bayboard released a cascade that exposed the top of what could be a low cupboard at the base of the back wall.

'Odd spot for a cat-flap.' David hauled out the penultimate bayboard.

I was too tense for speech. Intuitively I knew that it wasn't a cupboard door, and what lay behind it. And I knew to a fraction of an inch the width of David's shoulders. We cleared the rest in a breathless silence, then crawled in. The door was the size of a cupboard under the average sink, and so warped that he couldn't pull it open by the wooden handle. He rapped it with the heel of a small steel chisel. The raps rang hollow.

'Couple of torches in my pocket, love. Either'll do. Get one whilst I prise this open.'

I was quick but he had it open before I was back with a small, flattish, black-leathered torch. 'Which of these three buttons is the switch?'

'Middle. Thanks.' He blinked in the strong beam. 'Let's have it.' He lay on his face and I peered over his shoulders as he played the light into the hidden recess. It went back for another four or five feet, was the same width and height as the log-store with walls and roof of the same rough brick, but it had an old wooden floor with a trapdoor. Not much bigger than the one to the loft, it had a rusted iron handle and hinges.

'Give me elbow room, Rosie. Thanks.' David squeezed and edged through on his elbows and crouched on his knees to open the trap. It opened easily, soundlessly. I was half through and rested on my elbows as he shone the light on narrow-walled, rough-hewn stone steps curving down to a low, blackened door that had a spatula-shaped, medieval wooden latch and a large rusty iron bolt that looked open.

'Bingo,' he said.

I breathed very carefully. Jody was standing across my back, stiffening as at a rat-hole. I smelt them too. I swallowed. 'Life is full of little surprises.'

'As I'll bet the pygmies that built this said when they tried to get their first barrel down. Or was this just a bolt-hole for when the Excise blokes came calling?'

'Probably. Unless there's another way out from below.'

'Figures.' He tried but could not get even one shoulder through. Wrenching free, he lowered his head to listen. I

162

held my breath and heard only Jody's panting. He raised his head. 'Pongs of rodents and mould.'

My throat was tight. I told myself savagely to stop being a rip-roaring neuro. 'Shift out and let me in. I can get down. So can she, and if I go ahead she won't push me over. Once down I'll open that door and let her flush them out before I go in.' David was trying again. 'Stop trying to decapitate yourself, man! You'll never get through that.'

His head came up like a cork from a bottle. 'All I need is a good saw. Henry Gillon should have one. Won't take long to knock him up and –'

'Have Maria here like a bat out of hell. That we don't need. All we need is to know what else is down there. We must – and if I scream my head off, I scream my head off. Shift out and let me get on with it.'

He hesitated for several seconds. 'Right. Back right out with her. We'll want both torches. Something to show you.'

I opened my mouth to speak, changed my mind and did as he said. When he had followed us out, I closed the door. 'Show or tell, David?'

'Both.' He got his second torch. 'All I heard just now was bugger-all. No scrabbling, rustling.' Jody was snuffling and scratching at the foot of the closed door. 'They must've smelt her and beat it.'

'She's still smelling them.'

'Oh, aye.' He looked at the door as if he had it under a microscope. 'Sure as hell no one got down this way while that was loaded and –'

'There's no sign of another way down from outside and if there were Maria would know about it. So would all Littlehythe.' He just looked at me. 'You think there is?'

He said, 'Just thinking of the crafty buggers that built this. I'll show you how these operate.' He gave me one torch and demonstrated on his. Both were the size of a packet of cigarettes, but much heavier. On the upper, flat side were David's initials on a metal strip and on the reverse, three tiny red buttons in a row. 'Press all three simultaneously,' he went on, 'and you're in business whether the light's on or off. Repeat to switch the lot off. Range approx. five hundred yards.'

'Handy.'

'Yep. We use roughly similar types on the job. I had these two made up to my specifications and brought them back to prevent their going AWOL in my absence.'

'And just brought them along for the ride?'

'Why not? Good torches. Clear?'

I looked at his face. 'Yes. And on why the Yanks and BCC are fighting for you. You draw a classy blueprint.'

He flushed. 'Like hell I do! Standing back and literally dropping you in it.'

'Cool it, my love.' I patted his face. 'Not your fault your lot came over in long-boats and mine were at the receiving end and did very nicely out of it.'

He kissed me quickly, passionately. 'Just don't break your bloody neck on those steps. I'll light you down.'

I slid feet first through the trap that was just wide enough for shoulders a couple of inches broader than mine and with my left hand caught Jody's collar as she slithered after me. I held her just behind me. The steps were slippery with damp that glistened in our torchlights, the patches of mould on the walls had the deathly whiteness of fungus that had never known sunlight and

Murdo's wizened, staring-eyed face in the yard last night. There were only nine steps and at every step down the smell grew more throttling. The steps ended a couple of feet from the old door and the ground was unevenly bricked. Jody yelped, and scratched the door excitedly. The bolt was open but the door stayed shut.

I glanced back at David's shadowy face above the light in his extended right hand. 'I'll give them a few seconds to beat it again, then try the latch. If that doesn't do it, I'll try and kick it open.' Somehow my voice sounded normal. I didn't feel normal. I felt terrified.

'Why not try a shove first? If it's warped or blocked from within, why bust a toe?'

'Right.' I pushed the latch up and down and as neither made any difference, used my right shoulder on the door. It fell open so rapidly that I stumbled inwards over Jody, who was yelping and trying to struggle free. My instincts made me cling to her as I righted us both. I didn't hear the door shutting behind us but I heard the soft slither of an oiled bolt and pressed all three buttons as a man's voice whispered, 'Keep your trap shut – hold her good – put out that light or she gets it first.'

My torchlight and terror of rats went out together. I knew that voice. So did Jody. And as she always trusted her friends, her instincts took such a beating that it was a few seconds before she stopped struggling and her hackles stiffened round my clutching hand. I stared into the darkness and whispered, 'What now, Kevin?'

I heard his quick intake of breath. 'You're sharp. Best mind you don't cut yourself.' His whisper sounded as if he was smiling. It wasn't a nice sound. A torch came on behind me and the light fell on an open, empty camp-bed against the wall on my left. 'Get along that bed, sit if you fancies, but hold her good and you'll neither come to no harm. I'm not stopping.'

I had known since I heard the bolt closing that there was another way out. I knew now where it must come out and why he hadn't used it immediately he heard us overhead. David and I might not have seen him, but Jody would have let us know. My bringing her down here was the break he needed. I moved with her to the bed. I didn't sit. 'May I turn?' I asked.

'Suit yourself.'

I tightened my grip on Jody's collar and turned slowly. She hunched to spring and gave a low growl, but I was able to restrain her as the shotgun under his right arm was pointed at her and not me. I said slowly, clearly, as if to a tiresome child, 'Stop messing about with that shotgun, Kevin. You know dead well that if you blow off her head you'll have to blow off mine and your dad won't like that at all.'

He didn't answer at once, but he slightly lowered the double-barrelled muzzle. His right hand was on the trigger; his left held the torch with the beam directed at my feet to illuminate but not startle Jody. She watched him under her eyelids and was now ominously still and silent. That didn't bother him. He knew I could control her unless he attacked me, and that I knew he was one of the best shots on the marsh: if I risked suddenly blinding him with my torchlight, he could kill us both with his eyes shut. He looked about sixteen in the shadowy darkness behind the light, but exuded the self-assurance of a dangerously conceited man. Straight-backed, with his curly head tilted to the right, his bulky fishing-jacket hanging open over a dark rollneck and jeans, he stood with his booted feet a little apart. His outfit told me where else he had been last night; his shadowy face, and above all his stance, told me so much more that I had the ambivalent sensation of something akin to relief. It was my stance, and had been my cousin Robert's when listening hard and thinking fast in tight corners. Right now he could be my or Robert's younger brother, and that it didn't seem to add up only meant I had my figures wrong. What did add up was that I was not dealing with an alien intelligence. Just an evil intelligence I had met before.

At last he said in his normal voice, 'What my dad don't know won't hurt him.' He jerked his head upwards. 'Why's he gone quiet?'

'As I'm not screaming R.A.T.S., I'll bet he's nipped back to the kitchen for a quick smoke. We left the kitchen window open,' I lied very slowly. David needed time. So did I. My eyes had grown acclimatised to the surrounding darkness and I could make out the outline of the low door in the wall behind him and a large grip dumped against it. 'I smell them but can't hear any. You put down poison?'

'Yeah.' He was still listening keenly. 'Best hold her, hadn't you?'

'Yes. Thanks for the tip. Mind telling me what you're doing down here on what's now my property – or haven't you heard?'

'I heard.' That could have come from Walt. I could weep for Walt. But not now. 'You don't want to know nothing, miss. You wants to sit nice and quiet till Mr Lofthouse fetches you out. He's not stupid – me, neither. He's not having no quick drag. He's gone up Mr Gillon's for a saw like he says.' He began backing cautiously. 'You'll pardon me not stopping.'

'Of course.' He was taking a calculated risk. I did the same. 'If David's gone, it's for the nearest phone. That's in Potts and his car's there. You can't hang about and risk being picked up by the cops with last night's catch in your jacket and what's in that grip.' He stopped on his back foot. 'If he hasn't gone you can lay every quid you picked up night-fishing he's waiting at the wellhead with a log in each hand, and since you can't tote that grip in your teeth and will need your free hand to open the bolts holding down whatever the cover's nailed on, you'll be the sitting duck he was when you got him with the poker in Duncan's cottage.' He had stopped on both feet. 'Was that your idea or Duncan's? Obviously Duncan was in on it,' I went on chattily, 'but my money's on you. Only someone with your intelligence could have thought up spraying scent like mine around. That was a brilliant touch, Kevin.'

He was a good actor. Robert had been a superb one.

'Know your trouble, Miss Rose? You seen too much telly. I dunno what you going on about. I never done Mr Lofthouse.' He packed exactly the right measure of injured innocence into his voice. 'You ask Sam Parker and old Biffer and they'll tell you I was on me bike coming home for me tea when Mr Lofthouse copped it. And I not done no fishing last night – up Astead with me mates I was, and they'll tell you gone three afore I come back here to fetch what's rightly mine and get in a bit of mushrooming for old Ma Burt as opens Coxden stores of a Sunday morning and says she can take all I fetches her.'

'I'll bet she can. We're having a marvellous crop this year.' (And David, seeing Kevin close to in daylight for the first time in three years yesterday morning, developed an allergy to mushrooms. He hadn't forgotten I never ate cooked breakfasts. He had a phenomenal memory, especially for faces. But he had to prove a theory before he would voice it, even to me.) 'Actually, Kevin, your dad told me a couple of hours back that you were spending the night in Astead.' I paused intentionally. In his place I would now expect to be told that Murdo was dead, be reappraising my own situation and want to know just how much I knew. So would Robert. He had never taken unnecessary chances or wasted good opportunities. Robert wouldn't prompt me now. Nor did Kevin. 'Nice night for a rave.' I added casually. 'Even better for a little quiet fishing off Midstreet whilst Endel was empty and Duncan and Co. getting themselves a cast-iron alibi in Cliffhill. Very snazzy timing – and that was a very snazzy spiel, Kevin! Nice work!'

He was in Robert's class as an actor. He laughed. 'No offence, miss, but if you not seen too much telly you gone soft in the head! Like I says – beats me what you're on about.'

I had been watching Jody out of the corner of my eye and her ears had shot up. I had to get the torchlight higher. 'Diamonds, duckie.' I blinked in the sudden glare. 'Get that light out of my eyes, Kevin. I can't think straight if I can't see straight –' He lowered the beam to my neck. 'Thanks. Where was I?'

'Talking a right load of –'

'Come off it!' I smiled. 'I'm an Endel. Smuggling built Endel and is in our blood.' I wasn't sure, but I had the impression his figure stiffened. 'Of course I can smell it when it's going on – and it usually is – down our way. We all can, and I'd lay Endel the only people in St Martin's who don't know you've been doing a nice little part-time job for Duncan for the past year are your family. I hope he's paid you well. And turned a blind eye to the stone or two you've nicked from every catch before delivery. You've earned all you could get: without you to close mouths Duncan and his chums would've been nicked months ago.'

He dropped part of the act, but not his guard. He had to know why I had neither mentioned Murdo nor explained talking to Walt two hours ago. 'No skin off your nose, then?'

I shook my head slowly. 'I just object very strongly to incomers exploiting local talents and muscling in on old marsh customs. Smuggling's our business, not theirs. We've been bringing in brandy, baccy, laces, tea – you name it, so long as the price is right – for centuries.' I looked openly around the darkened cellar. The door behind him was a little to his left and against the wall that was now on my left and his right, was a wooden rack. I nodded at it and sniffed loudly. 'Yes. Cidery. That's where old Ginny stored her apples, isn't it?' He nodded slightly and I felt him watching me like a hunter with his prey in his sights. 'And at other times, others stashed their loot down here till the heat was off. Made to measure for them – and you. Wasn't it?' I didn't wait for his answer. I had to say more to get more out of him. 'You couldn't hide yours at home. Your mum would have found it, told your dad, and he wouldn't wear that, even for you.' Again, I paused deliberately. He was a cold-blooded killer and dangerous as a rabid dog, but he loved his parents and especially Walt. Robert had loved our grandfather; Grandfather, from all accounts and from his actions, had loved his elder son and Robert. 'But, as you've said, what they don't know can't hurt them and I'm sure you could trust old Ginny to turn a blind eye and keep her hands off the wads of readies you couldn't shove into a bank or post office. People ask questions when someone on agricultural wages starts shovelling in stacks of old notes. I've heard the old girl fancied you rotten since you were a kid.'

'You don't want to believe all you hears.'

'Dead right! I don't. I never swallowed Duncan's spiel about your uncle lending Harry a faulty van. I'm certain those brakes were fine till you did a quick job on them when Harry was in here Friday evening. Classy bit of quick thinking that, Kevin. Must've given you a nasty turn seeing the van outside, knowing your goodies were down here and wanting them to stay put until you'd collected tonight's catch. Naturally you had to come back for them now as the rest of the stuff is due to be cleared later this morning. I suppose Duncan told you this when you rang him at the Blacks' to say "catch landed" or whatever, though I don't suppose you told him you wouldn't be delivering and were doing a runner as –'

'S'pose what you like!' he spat contemptuously and began backing again. 'No skin off my nose.'

I had to delay him. Jody's head and ears were cocked on the door behind him and he had a gun. 'Just like my father. Fascinating how Endel family history repeats itself.'

He stopped; involuntarily, I sensed. 'What's that to me?'

'He was your age when he did a runner from Endel. And he had a pretty good reason too. His father and brother had tried to drown him in Midstreet main almost exactly where later, my cousin Robert tried to drown me. And –'

'You're having me on and I'm not –'

'Like hell I am! Stuck in the groove, us Endels, aren't we, Cousin Kevin? Or didn't poor old Ginny tell you she was your natural gran before you shoved her into Littlemarsh main?'

He hissed like a snake, Jody bared her teeth and I needed all my strength to hold her back. 'Bleeding, lying old bitch! Swore on her bible she'd never told none and had me swearing and I never and I'm glad as I done –' he stopped in time – 'like I swore! I'll not have it said as my dad –'

'Belt up and listen, Kevin!' I snapped authoritatively and silenced him only because he had been indoctrinated into respecting Endel authority before he shed his milk teeth. But I knew it wouldn't take him more than seconds to hit back, so I wasted none. 'Ginny never told me. No one has. No one would dare! I own Endel, employ a lot of local labour, and even if I look a soft touch no one with any sense who's known the Endels would push their luck on that one! We haven't hung on to our land for over four hundred years without knowing how to play rough and dirty – but you have to have Endel blood to know just how rough and dirty we'll play. And as like recognises like – I guessed you had our blood before I turned just now and saw you holding that gun on us and knew it! Then – now – you could be my or Robert's brother. And you don't just look like an Endel, you think and act like one. So do I! That's how I know you're about to do a runner to Holland or somewhere – in your place, that's what I'd do. And though I wouldn't have murdered three pepole to keep their mouths shut, that's what our cousin Robert, Grandad and God alone knows how many of our Endel forefathers would have done, were they you. I'll bet our grandad would have been dead proud of you for being such a right chip off the old block – but not your dad. He doesn't know you killed Ginny and Max Jones but he knows you killed Murdo last night. I know you killed all three. You had to, whether or not they got greedy or just nosy. Only sure way of shutting their mouths.'

He said in a tight, hard voice, 'Proper little know-all, aren't you, Rosie? Know your real trouble? You talks too much.'

'So do you, lad! Drop that gun!' David's voice cracking out of the lightless torch in my right hand startled us both for a split-second. It was all Jody needed. She sprang free with a force that sent me staggering backwards as simultaneously Kevin fired and David catapulted through the door behind him. David flung himself over me as Jody's weight toppled Kevin backwards and the second barrel fired. When the second retort faded the only sounds in the darkness were the thudding of David's and my hearts. And before either of us recovered our breath or moved, we knew what had happened.

'What's going on down there? Who's there?' Henry Gillon's muffled bellow came from above. 'Open that door immediately or I call the police!'

David rolled off me and shouted. 'David Lofthouse, Henry! Wait!' He switched on his torch, picked up and returned mine, then crouched by the silent heap on the floor a few feet away. Jody's spring had knocked the muzzle upwards and backwards. Her inert, mutilated body lay sprawled across Kevin's and the muzzle was embedded in what remained of his chest. I leant one hand on David's shoulder and looked down in an agony I had not known since my mother died. I stooped to touch

Jody, but David caught my hand. 'No, love, no. Not till the cops get here.' He stood up, put an arm round my shoulders and drew me away. Unbolting the inner door, he shone his torchlight on the steps to avoid blinding Henry's face peering through the trap. 'Get the police here fast, Henry. Tell them there's been a fatal shooting accident in this cellar and they can get down through the well and should bring a saw to enlarge that trap. Rose and Jody caught an intruder down here and the bloke shot Jody before his own gun got him.'

Before Henry could answer, Maria's voice wailed. 'Oh, no! Not Jody! Oh Rose – darling – are you all right?'

David called quickly, 'Rose is safe, Maria. She can get up this way – coming up now. Take care of her. I'll wait for the cops down here. Tell them we've touched nothing, Henry.'

'Right away, David. Just see Rose up first. Any idea who the chap is – was?'

I said quickly and mechanically, 'Kevin Ames. Next of kin, father, Walt Ames, Endel Farm, Midstreet 109. I'm not coming up till the police get here. Hurry, Henry, please.'

He did. Fifteen minutes later PC Curtis arrived from Coxden. The two CID men from Astead took a little longer. One was Detective Sergeant Brand and the other a Detective Chief Inspector Donkin wearing a jacket and grey tie instead of the blazer and open shirt he had worn at the concert.

TEN

THE LETTER FROM THE DEAD HAD BEEN WRITTEN ON the last Monday in May, but never posted. Mr Yates, the youngish master builder who had begun repairing Ferry that morning, handed it to me at the front door of my flat on the evening of the last Monday in June.

'One of my lads found this under a board edging the hearth this afternoon, Mrs Endel, and having to come down the marsh to look at Frank Wattle's main stack up the Crown, I thought I'd drop it in.'

'Thanks very much, Mr Yates.' I accepted the small, cheap brown, thickish and grubby envelope, feeling as if I'd been kicked hard in the stomach. 'How did it get there?'

He smiled cheerfully. 'You'd not ask if you'd taken up as many floors in old buildings as I have. We're always finding old letters, snaps, bits of jewellery, coins and the like that have slipped down between rotting boards unnoticed and lain there since no telling when. I reckon old Ginny wrote it and put it aside to stamp and it slipped down and slipped her mind. She was much of my old mum's age. She's always putting things down and forgetting what she done with 'em.'

'Must've been that. Won't you come in, Mr Yates?'

'Ta, no, seeing I've a job waiting and you got company.' He glanced at General Wenden's car then up at the heavy rainclouds. The weather had changed along with so much more and it had just stopped raining for the first time since David got back from the States last Friday. 'More coming from that sky, so more inside work I got for my lads the better. But now we started I'll not fetch them off Ferry till we finish the job in the three to four weeks.' He chuckled. 'Can't be too soon for Mrs Gillon. Can't wait to get her hands on it soon as you and her hubby exchange contracts, from what she was telling me this morning.' He backed down a few steps to give the roof an expert survey. He looked tough enough to have put it up single-handed. 'Tell you this, Mrs Endel, puttin' old Ferry to rights is a mite easier than the job we did for you on old Endel.' He cocked his head at a distant outburst of childish cheering. 'Kiddies sound like they're enjoying it.'

I smiled. 'Wheelchair racing in the hall as it's too wet outside. Thanks again, Mr Yates.'

'No trouble. 'Evening.'

I went on smiling until I closed the front door. Then I leant against it and looked at the envelope for a few seconds; I left it unopened on my office desk and went back to the sitting room. 'Sorry about that, General. Just Yates with a message. Do sit down and have another sherry.'

'Not for me, thanks, m'dear. One's my ration when driving.' He lowered himself back on the sofa beside me and David returned to his armchair. 'Must be off, shortly. My man's missus doesn't like me late for supper. Off again tomorrow, eh, Lofthouse? Good God, man, you fly the Atlantic more often than I drive to Astead. Fourth time in under two weeks, eh?'

'By this time tomorrow, sir.'

'How long's this posting?'

David glanced at me. 'That's still to be arranged, sir. I hope not too long.'

'Hmmm. Don't imagine you'll be sorry to leave our rain. How's it affecting the farm, Rose?'

'Walt says doing nothing but good providing it doesn't keep on much longer. It's holding up cutting the clover.'

'Dodgy crop, clover, but from the look of yours when I drove by, waiting a few more days won't hurt.' He gave me one of his piercing glances. 'Good man, Walt. How do you find him?'

I shrugged. 'Outwardly, as ever.'

'So they tell me. Putting up the very good show one would expect from him. Nevertheless –' the lines deepened on his rigid teak face – 'a very bad show that business, and a very hard knock to any father. Still, a bit of weight off his mind the chaps giving his brother's van a clean bill. My man tells me he's known more than a few brakes give without warning from fair wear and tear. You met that, Lofthouse?'

'Not personally. I've heard of it happening.'

'Just so. They tell me you're keeping the Rover.'

'Yes. Rose is letting me keep it here until I've settled matters my end.'

'Sound scheme. Plenty of room here.' He glanced at the foot of the closed door that shut out the children's voices. 'Too much, eh, m'dear?' I nodded slightly. 'You must get another good dog. You mustn't live here alone in winter without one.' He appealed to David. 'Agree, Lofthouse?'

'Yes, sir.'

I said, 'Later, not yet.'

David looked at the floor, General Wenden at my face. 'Know how you feel, gal – been through it – only solution is bite the bullet and get an immediate replacement. You must take action on that – and Walt Ames. He's a hardy man but no youngster. The pack he's carrying would break many a younger man. It could crack his health and you'd have the devil of a job finding a replacement of his calibre.'

'General, I know that, but –' I spread my hands helplessly – 'what can I do?'

David said, 'What would you do, sir?'

'If he were one of my men, Lofthouse?' David nodded. 'Mmmm. Two courses open. One. Pack him straight off on a long compassionate leave. Two. Straight back into action in the front line. On deliberation, I'd go for the second.' He looked at me. 'You can't prise a good farmer from his land and livestock at this time of year and expect him to stand easy – or expect that of any man if you pull up his roots, and particularly not a marshman.' Unusually, he hesitated. 'Have you told him you've no thought of replacing him?'

I looked at him incredulously. 'Of course not. He knows as long as I own Endel his job and his home are his for life.'

'Just so. Nevertheless – hmmm – my man tells me there's been careless talk around that you're unlikely to renew his contract.'

I was so angry I momentarily forgot the unopened

letter. 'That's monstrous and must be stopped! I'll put Walt, then Marlene and Daph, straight on this, first thing tomorrow. Stamp it out in Shepland for me, please.'

'Will do, m'dear.'

'Thank you – and for telling me.'

'Didn't enjoy it, but much enjoyed this pleasant interlude. Time I was off – no, no, don't stir yourself, Rose. See you're upset – would've upset m'wife – couldn't take careless talk. You'll see me back out, eh, Lofthouse? Many thanks for the sherry, Rose. Before I go – how's young Tom Bagley shaping in your garden?'

'Very well. Now working full time.'

'Good show. Sound lad, I'm told. Might trust him with my roses when he's more experienced. Roses need experience. Miss old Murdo's. Glad you've put him with the Endels. Your father would have done the same. Right, Lofthouse.'

He stooped through the doorway that cleared his own head by two inches. David gave me a searching glance and followed him out. I stayed on the sofa thinking of the old man's unyielding loyalty to old friends and old soldiers, of roses, and of the exquisite scent in the Gillons' dining room that overlooked their rose garden on that Sunday morning after another night David and I would never forget or bear to remember.

The bells of St Mary's, Littlehythe were ringing for 8 a.m. Holy Communion when Henry ushered us in, waited for Maria to hand round our tea, then left with her, closing the door behind them. Ten minutes earlier, just before the two CID men came on from Ferry, Maria told me Nora had called on her way to church and wanted to speak to me in the hall.

Nora, in Sunday black, her eyes red-rimmed, grasped my hands. 'Just had to see for meself you're all right, miss – Mrs Henry's told me and I'm ever so sorry and'll not say more than I hope as you didn't mind me ringing Mr Henry when I see back of Mr Lofthouse head over the hedge and didn't know what to think – and Mr Henry always said any time I'm worried and –'

'Nora, dear, I'm thankful you did. You were a god-send.' I kissed her cheek. I had thawed only superficially and beneath the ice was solid. 'God bless you for it.'

Maria was back, her eyes bright with compassionately contained curiosity, her hair in a black-bowed ponytail, her short-sleeved white shirt loose over black jeans. 'Nora, dear, the bells have started and here's a police car.'

Once more, within a few hours, three men sitting with me round a table. Once more David and I repeating our initial accounts, sticking to the provable truth and omitting the unprovable. But this time, in turn, dictating our statements to Detective Sergeant Brand, with Detective Chief Inspector Donkin listening in silence and watching us from the head of the table. He had seated Brand on his left; me, then David, on his right; and it was clear they had done their homework on him. Neither detective queried David's explanation that he had told me before we left Endel for Ferry that he had heard from a reliable source he refused to name now, but would under oath, that the police suspected uncut diamonds were being smuggled in probably through Midstreet Marsh. It was only after we signed our statements that their impeccably polite and formal attitudes relaxed fractionally. DCI Donkin took out of his jacket pocket a small plastic bag half filled with what appeared to be little pebbles and trickled a few out on to the clean blotter Henry had placed at the head of the highly polished light oak dining table. He saw my eyes widen. 'Never seen uncut diamonds before, madam?'

'No, Chief Inspector. I thought they'd look like little chunks of dirty glass.'

'I expect you did, madam. How about you, sir?'

'No,' said David. 'I've seen others. A mining mate showed me some when I did a two-year stint in Australia for my firm.' He looked across the table. 'Want names, places, dates, Sergeant?'

DS Brand put his ballpoint on his open notebook and thumbed back his fair forelock. He was an Astead man of around David's age and build, with a strong, good-natured face. 'I don't think we need that now, Dr Lofthouse.'

David nodded and returned his attention to the blotter. 'Gem, or industrial, Chief Inspector?'

'Hard to say at this stage, but we have reason to suspect gem.'

David said, 'Odds-on.'

I looked at him for the first time since we had sat down. Maria had provided us with hot baths and clean shirts; David with Henry's razor and a clean adhesive dressing to replace the filthy strip he had pulled off before washing his hair. His hair was still damp, his clean-shaven, faintly bruised face still taut, and the anger still lingered at the back of his eyes. 'Gem more valuable?' I asked.

'Infinitely. It would hardly be worth the sweat of running uncut industrials into London. It's not a major cutting centre, just a secondary. Paying a bent expert cutter would eat into the small profits.' He turned to Donkin. 'May I ask if you know the bloke?'

'No harm in asking, sir.' The gravelly London voice was gentle, but there was no gentleness in the heavy face and hard little eyes. 'You might say we have a suspect under surveillance. Know much about diamonds, then?'

'No. Just the little I picked up from my mining mate. May I also know how many the lad had on him?'

'I don't see why not. Forty-three in all. Twenty in a little leather bag. The rest in a sock.'

'Oh, aye.' David's face was expressionless. 'If they're good carat that explains his gun.'

My ice was too solid for even a scratch on the surface. 'Worth so much?' All three men nodded. 'How much?'

'What would you say, sir?'

David shook his head. 'I wouldn't, Chief Inspector. I don't know enough about the current European diamond market and current prices to speculate on a valuation. But if I'm right in presuming these reached Holland from South Africa –' he paused enquiringly and the other man nodded again – 'as it's a reasonable assumption they'd only bother to send what they anticipate are good carat that distance, I'd be interested in your approximate figure, if you'd care to give it.'

'I expect you would, sir. Well, now –' Donkin flicked over a couple of the pebbles with a thick forefinger. 'If they're all good carat, the stones we removed from the pockets of the deceased's fishing-jacket might well fetch around thirty to thirty-five thousand on the open market. A fence would pay less than half the market value, but not much less.'

'Handy sum. What would be his rate for the job?'

Donkin and Brand exchanged impassive glances. The

latter took over. 'No saying with any certainty yet, Dr Lofthouse, but from the cash we found on him and amongst the clothes in his grip, he didn't do badly.' He consulted his notebook. 'We also removed from the deceased's pockets a wallet containing twenty old one-pound notes and fifteen shillings and threepence in loose change. We removed five hundred and ninety-two old oncers from his grip.'

I froze solid. David glanced at me then asked, 'Do you know who paid him the cash?'

Donkin smiled benignly with his lips. 'We have reason to believe so, sir, but until we have completed our inquiries – which shouldn't take too long – I think we'll leave it there.' He faced me. 'As you own Endel Farm, madam, I have to inform you we will be requesting a search warrant to search the premises later today, and that your tenant Mr Walter Ames has already informed us he has no objection to our doing so without a warrant any time we see fit.'

I thanked God for the ice. 'Thank you, but I knew this. It was the only thing Mr Ames said to me when you kindly let me see him back to his car alone. All I said to him was that you can search Endel House and the outhouses any time you like without a warrant. I should have said so sooner. I'm sorry. I forgot.'

'No harm done, madam. Thank you for your co-operation.' He paused thoughtfully. 'Mr Ames informed us he has worked on your farm since a lad, so would I be right in thinking you know him well?'

'Yes. He's been my farm manager for the last four years and I couldn't have a better. I like him very much and trust him implicitly.'

'That's nice to hear, madam. Yes – well now – we'll be

having another talk with Mr Ames later today after he and his wife have had a little time to themselves, and from what you've just said, he may be able to help us.'

I looked straight into his hard little eyes. 'I know he will if he can, but I'm very sure he can't help you much and that he had no idea Kevin was involved in all this. He took the shock quietly, as he takes everything quietly. I'm absolutely certain that had he known, he would have stopped it, quietly and legally.'

'Is that so, madam? Yes. You may well be right. Sons don't tell their dads much these days – if they ever did. It's their mums that hear most and what they don't hear they guess, more often than not, rightly.' I was shaking my head. 'You don't think the lad's mum spotted anything?'

'If she had she'd have told her husband. He's her oracle and they're devoted to each other.'

'That's nice for them. 'Specially now.' He was almost human. 'Nasty shock for parents. But I'm just wondering how it would have been if the lad spun his mum a yarn about winning on the pools and asked her not to tell his dad because he was saving his winnings for something special his dad wouldn't approve.'

'Mrs Ames would still have told her husband and he would want to know which pool and how much.'

'You might be right, madam.'

I said nothing.

David, watching Donkin over his glasses, picked up the cue I had missed. 'Do you know if Duncan Morgan won on the pools?'

The atmosphere relaxed more. Brand smiled faintly. 'If he did, it wasn't under that name.'

David nodded noncommittally. 'Presumably you know he's got form.'

Donkin said, 'We know now, sir. We don't go looking for these things unless we have to, but when we do we generally find what we're looking for.' He turned back to me. 'Young Kevin Walter Ames had none. Lively, well-liked lad from all accounts and not the first decent lad to fall in with bad company. But he shouldn't have had that gun and used it on your dog, madam. I'm sorry he did that. Not nice, shooting a dog, even if, as you've stated, you thought him too startled to know what he was doing.'

The ice cracked and tears poured down my face, but I managed to control my voice. 'I'm sure he was. She sprang on him before the first barrel fired, and as either he dropped the torch or she knocked it out of his hand and it went out, it was all so dark and quick I'd no idea if it was Kevin or her weight that fired the second. There seemed only a second or two between the retorts.'

David said, 'As I've stated, at the most three seconds.' He edged my untouched tea towards me. I dried my face. For a few minutes no one spoke and the room was filled with silence and the scent of roses.

No, it hadn't taken the police long, I reflected, sitting on the sofa, looking at the large vase of long-stemmed red roses Marlene had arranged and set in the empty hearth this morning. But Jody's death had left such a gap in my life and my heart that that first week without her had seemed interminable. By that Monday evening, however, all the Morgan Consort but Harry were helping the police with their inquiries and my telephone line was red hot.

'Darling, how are you both? ... Yes. I just can't believe Duncan ... poor darling Mama would have been shattered! ... And the Blacks – of course, I've never thought them our sort, but nothing like this! Only Henry says ... But I refuse to believe that nice Christine ... You and David don't? I must tell Henry! Poor sweetie, he's shattered! He's always liked Frank Cross and that poor boy, Harry – you've heard the police want to interview him soon as the doctors allow? ... You don't think they knew, either? I can't wait to tell Henry ... I always thought Kevin Ames a sweetie – his poor parents! Poor you! I know what she meant to you ... Yes, darling, I know you don't want to talk about her – but how will you cope without her?'

'Rose – do forgive my not ringing till now but I haven't had a moment since taking out David's stitches in morning surgery. ... Why haven't you asked Father to give you something to help you through this? ... Well, perhaps – one needs a clear mind ... God, yes! Knocked me for six! All in top form at Saturday night's party – then this – even Chris ... I just can't believe she ... What's that? You don't? David doesn't ... He thinks she needs a good lawyer? ... Yes! You're right! We've been old chums since Benedict's and she hasn't been here long enough to make many friends outside the hospital. I must rally round. I'll ring Edward now! But first, I have to give you some advice. You must get another guard-dog. David said in surgery that he's wangled just over another week then must get back on the job. I can't take the thought of you in Endel without one – not on top of everything else – Dear, brave, stubborn, little Rose! I'm going to come back to you on this ...'

'Rose! We're devastated! How are you both? ... How

could we have let Duncan pull the wool over our eyes all these years? Honestly, one can't trust anyone these days . . .'

'Rose, we're so distressed for you and that wretched boy's parents . . . I expect you've heard . . . Oh, no, no! Not our dear Duncan . . . that very nice couple . . . we've bought a couple of rather good pieces from them at very fair prices . . . known Frank Cross years – incorruptible as the Bank of England . . . The police must be mistaken! They're always arresting the wrong people and failing to arrest the right – read any newspaper – and they still haven't got David's attacker . . .'

David was sitting on my bed when I took that last call. 'Our Dunk knew his public,' he said, replacing the receiver.

On that Wednesday morning, both inquests in Astead brought in identical verdicts: 'Death by misadventure'. That afternoon, Christine and Frank Cross, having been cautioned, were allowed to return to their normal lives; Harry had recovered sufficiently to be told by police they would not be pressing charges against him; Duncan and Stephen and Sandra Black were charged with smuggling uncut diamonds, refused bail and remanded in custody for one week, and a new marsh legend was born. 'Thirty-odd thousand in diamonds – six hundred in cash – and he was only twenty-one!'

On that Friday morning, Kevin's funeral and no standing room left in St Martin's parish church; that afternoon, Marlene, Daph, Maria, Henry and David sitting with me in the Endel pew in the little Saxon church on the loneliest part of Midstreet Marsh; General Wenden reading the lesson; the greying members of the local British Legion escorting Murdo's coffin to the old graveyard backed against the southern wall and edged by a long narrow dyke. There were no formally planted yews and shrubs, the few small paths were roughly scythed, the majority of the ancient graves hidden under thick timothy grass, and all the old and newer granite headstones wind-pitted and sunken at odd angles in the boggy turf. The sky was alive with birds; the bright, warm, salty air with birdsong and the soft sighing of the sea.

We dined with the Gillons that night. Driving us back, David said, 'Best spot I've seen for waiting out eternity, but posterity'll beat no path to poor old Murdo's grave. Unlike our Kev's.' His tone hardened. 'Flowers'll be fresh for generations on the local lad that made it good. Not one dry eye amongst the neighbours this morning, nor, I'd lay my all, one not raising a glass to him tonight.' He switched into broad Kent, 'Well, I mean can't hold it against the lad for doing what come natural and not as if he fetched in them nasty drugs as harm cruel. Diamonds don't harm none but insurance companies and the like and they got enough, haven't they? And seeing what he fetched in just the one haul – no saying what the young shaver not made if he been spared! Makes you think. Cruel waste and cruel shame he had to shoot the young lady of Endel's bitch and do hisself accidental, but like she told coroner, he was startled like and you can't expect an old head on young shoulders.' He paused, then added in his own voice, 'Puke-making, but the break his family and particularly old Walt can use.'

I had known when I got off the cellar floor that Jody had saved much more than my life with her own. I still couldn't bear talking about her, even to him, but that wasn't my only reason for taking time to speak. 'Yes.

Mrs Walt's main salvation is that John's her ewe lamb and that's helped by her detesting poor little Linda Burt and blaming her for leading Kevin astray. And if Nancy is pregnant, that'll help her still more. First grandchild.'

'John's wife? Who told you?'

'Marlene and Daph, just before they left after tea. They're sure she is.'

'Oh, aye. Help Walt too.'

I watched his shadowy, solid, profile. 'I hope so. He's in hell. Thank God he doesn't have to know it all.'

'He knew enough, love.'

'How?' I demanded. 'We've told no one.'

'He doesn't need to be told all, as he'll have worked most out for himself now he knows his white-headed lad was bent as a nine-bob note. The pathological evidence clinched both verdicts, but he knows Murdo's is a load of cobblers and though the coincidence of the twenty quid went unremarked in court, he won't have missed it. And as old Ginny must've known what Kev stashed in her cellar, it's bound to have crossed his mind that his lad may have had a hand in her very timely fatal accident. And from there, I think, he took another look at Max Jones's death. Now it's public that the poor sod had just finished a stretch for flogging stolen cars up north when he moved in on Dunk and got stuck in earning his reputation as a scrounging, loud-mouthed drunk, Walt'll have caught on to the high probability that someone may have had the nous to close it. Proven cause, alcohol plus sleeping tablets. Simple. Lace a bottle with sleeping tablets, leave it handy and no alcoholic will put it down till it's empty.' He stopped speaking to turn on to the coast road, then went on: 'I think that was another you got right – Max got greedy. And as Dunk knew his old mate, I think that will have crossed his mind before Kev hammered it home by clouting me. And if he had survived, Dunk would now be singing like a canary and not just to save his own skin. Kev broke their rules. Now he's out of the picture, being pros, Dunk, Steve and Sandra are playing strictly by them – which is one hell of a break for the other three.'

'Honour amongst thieves? Yuck!'

'Correction, Rose. Just keeping to company rules. Good pros don't grass. Old Norm said they'd always known they were up against good pros. Dunk and Co. are, so they'll now take whatever Crown Court hands out, be out again on good behaviour in a year or two, disappear discreetly, and then at well-timed intervals, reappear with new names in another arty-crafty village in another nice, empty part of the coast, start up more musical evenings and get back in business. My money's on Cornwall. Good way from Kent and lots of quiet isolated beaches down there.'

I said angrily, 'And antique shops, damn them! And Walt will still be in hell.'

'He's tough, love. He'll handle it in his own time.'

'But he couldn't handle those tapes. You have got rid of them?'

He hesitated, 'Temporarily, not permanently.'

'David, you promised –'

'That I'd deal with them. I have. While we were in Astead yesterday and you were with Edward Smith, I registered them to myself care of my Washington bank. Sorry – I can't destroy evidence, even for you. That it's superfluous, pro tem, is no guarantee it'll remain so.'

I sighed. 'I should've known you could no more do that than falsify a fact. I could. I'd have tied them to a brick and dropped them in Midstreet main on Monday night. Though so much on them is unprovable, they'd destroy Walt. All else aside, he adored old Mrs Ames, and to discover she wasn't his mother –'

'Hold it there, love! We've no proof she wasn't. Neither hearsay nor visual impressions is hard evidence.'

'Huh! The second was enough to put you off mushrooms.'

'His smile did that.'

'It was Robert's?'

'No. Yours.'

I said between my teeth. 'Go on.'

'It was when I opened your front door to him. He was on the top step holding out the trug and smiling exactly like you when you need the protective cover of your dumb, all-sugar, little dolly act. The light was bloody good, so I took a closer look, spotted the additional resemblance to Robert and went off mushrooms. I knew you wouldn't want them for breakfast and stalled because I had to think this through. I needed proof before pinning "bastard" on Walt, and we still do. Kevin may have thought he was blurting out the truth – I'd say he did – but how do we know the old girl told him the truth? How do we know it wasn't something she had kidded herself into believing to console herself for losing or abandoning her own baby – if she ever had one, which remains unproven.'

My temper exploded. 'Stuff the Galahad! We know she wasn't lying. He killed Jody.'

He said wearily, 'Sure as hell do you claim prerogatives for Endels, woman. Cool it and think straight. The country's stiff with men that kill and ill-treat dogs – never heard of the RSPCA? Come to that, never taken a good look over your neighbours? Or just Daph? Half St Martin's could be your near or distant relatives, and probably are. Whether or not Grandad put it about, it's highly improbable your mutual ancestors didn't take what they fancied in an isolated rural area largely dependent on Endels for their daily crust. And he was bloody startled – by – my – voice.' He spun out the words. 'That was the factual cause. Jody and his deaths, the factual effects.'

My anger evaporated. 'You've left out the third. I'm alive.'

'I know it.' He took a long breath. 'Leave it there. I'll stash the tapes in my bank vault first chance after I'm back on Tuesday. I have to make that date. Both sides have been bloody decent about my overstaying and I can't string them along beyond Tuesday. Postponing the hell of leaving you won't make it less hellish. No –' he stifled my attempted interruption – 'not that one tonight, my love. Some other time. Not tonight.'

David came back to the sitting room. 'How did Yates get you under the belt?' he asked.

I told him and we went on to the office. I gestured at the unopened envelope. 'She'd never written me before.'

He hitched up his glasses for a close look at the slightly shaky but clear, old-fashioned handwriting. 'Pre-first world war elementary school copybook. Not unlike my dad's.' He looked up. 'What's in it, Rosie?'

I sat heavily in my desk chair. 'How in hell can I know yet?'

'Christ, love, don't expect me to explain how your primordial perceptions can pick up the underlying reality of a situation as fast as the speed of light,' he protested. 'Mine aren't in your class.'

I flushed. 'You mean you've no Endel blood.'

He shook his head. 'Not now. Time was – not far back – when I would've pretended I meant that to avoid another set-to over your obsessive ancestral guilt. Not now a demonstration of the reliability of my own has made me think this one through. And as I've just said, mine aren't in your class.'

'Yours?' I queried incredulously. 'You're admitting to possessing something you can't prove?'

'I don't need to. It's long-proven genetic law that the primitive instincts exist and we've all inherited them from our nomadic ancestors who had to develop them to stay alive in a very dangerous natural world. They had to be highly perceptive of every hint of danger nature threw their way and learn how to interpret and handle what they saw, smelt or heard, to survive and beget us. But in the majority of the modern, civilised human race, those instincts and perceptions are buried so deep that it takes something like a violent shock, or the sudden awareness that our own life, or the lives of those we love, are in imminent danger to rocket them up to take over. As you're in the minority whose instincts are much less deep, you only have to be over-tired or stressed to start picking up like radar. You didn't get that from the Endels. You got that from ancestors running round in skins thousands of years before your lot got stuck in the mud of Midstreet. And they're in such good shape –' he smiled slightly – 'that – twenty-four hours after ferrying Dunk just before and after Lady G.'s made the third in one week and subconsciously picking up without interpreting Dunk's terror that two of the three might not have been natural deaths – one sniff of his mothball was enough for your mind to flash the association-cum-danger signal. No sweat. Just something you can do.'

I thought of Sandra Black's face in the moonlit twilight and the barn owl. I breathed out carefully. 'When did yours take over?'

He looked at me for a few seconds. He had cut down dramatically on smoking over this last weekend that had been too good for either of us to notice what the weather was doing, but he lit a cigarette now. 'On Dunk's floor. But I only started thinking it out after total recall. Of course, you remember what I said when I surfaced.'

I felt ill, but had to be honest. 'I hoped you didn't.'

He said gently, 'I've known that since I had recall, love. I didn't tell you as I didn't think you were ready to handle it, and, in retrospect, nor was I. To clear it up was one of my motives for wangling this weekend, and since I got back –' he stubbed out the cigarette – 'I've been waiting for the right moment. I hope I've my timing right, as this matters like hell to us both and I'm not taking off tomorrow leaving it in the dark.' He nodded at the envelope. 'The time-bomb can wait a few more minutes.'

I clasped my shaking hands in my lap. 'I'm in no hurry to open it.'

He blinked rapidly. 'Just listen, Rosie.' He put his hands in his trouser pockets. 'When I came to and heard you weighing into Dunk, though I felt as if my brains were spilling out of my ears, I knew instantly and precisely what had happened and could happen: i.e., I knew I was a dead loss to protect you – and Dunk was as much protection as a cold rice pudding. If the sod was still around you'd go down fighting but hadn't a chance in hell against a bloke armed with what he used on me who could kill you to stop you identifying him – and that if Dunk was involved it would help you to remind him that your murder would open up the biggest can of worms in the business.' He took a deep breath. 'It would. Old Norm would have every cop in the county on the job – which we now know was the last thing Dunk wanted. And, somehow, I knew it before I flaked out again. Then it blacked out until it came back with the rest just after Murdo and I got up that flagstone three mornings later and knowing how you would have taken it nearly pitched me into that bloody cavity.' The memory haunted his eyes and tightened his face. 'I had to let it ride until I had thought this out and then, as you now know, shoved it on a back burner. And that's the truth, my love. Believe me?'

I gave a long shuddering sigh of far more than relief. 'Yes. Now. You were right to stall. Earlier –' I shook my head – 'I was too sad and too damned angry and sickened by my Endel blood to have taken it as anything but your Galahad streak attempting a whitewash. Thanks for straightening me out.'

'Thanks, but I haven't finished the job. Take more?' I nodded. 'Good,' he said gravely, 'as this I've wanted to hand you for years.' He held up his right hand with the fist clenched then raised his thumb. 'A. Knowing you, I've always known that you – and from all I've heard of him, probably your father – have missed out on that killer gene. You could never kill in cold blood. You could only kill in hot blood either in self-defence or defending the life of someone helpless and relying on your sole protection. And that's not only because you're a very feminine woman and in common with the overwhelming majority of women – who have the hard sweat of giving birth to life – you're instinctively and passionately opposed to taking it. B.' He straightened his forefinger: 'it's also because you've got a hyper-protective streak that, C –' his third finger went up – 'I've always suspected you've inherited from your mother. She loved, raised and protected you single-handed and did a bloody fine job on her daughter. Yes. Hers too. *Ergo* – D.' Fourth finger up. 'You're not half, you're one-quarter Endel. Your father was the half. Your kids, one-eighth, like, just possibly, Nancy Ames's baby. E.' All five up. 'None of this affects your absolute right to maintain your decision that the Endel entail dies with you.' He dropped his hand to his side. 'I've always known you'll never alter that and even though I've been, and still am, more than willing to take the calculated risk, I've no right to ask or expect you to take it and I'll never do either.' He needed another long breath. 'That's one of the two requests I'll never make of you, Rosie, but there's another I must. Will you please stop trying to protect me from picking up my own bill for loving you. I pay mine. You pay yours. Understood?'

'Yes.'

'Thanks.' He picked up the envelope and offered it to me. 'You might also stop trying to stall this until I've gone tomorrow and open it whilst the dust settles.'

'You do a good demolition job, David.' I took it from him with shaking hands that steadied involuntarily as soon as I took out the two tightly folded smallish pages of lined paper written on both sides. The letter was correctly headed and dated, strewn with capital letters, erratically punctuated, with a few words underlined, and written in black ink with a dip-pen and in the writer's spoken English. It read:

196

Dear Miss Rose,

I am sorry to trouble you but being troubled
bad in my mind I reckon I best turn to you the
once more for all I never wished you to know 'till
I'm gone as I Named you to have my cottage in
my Will after my time come. I done that after
being in the hospital with my poorly chest and
already the mite troubled and it come to me you
be best placed to do what's best for it being Mr
Rosser's girl.

If Mr Rosser been spared I be turning to him
now seeing I always knew he would know for why
like I reckon you do for all you've never shown –
same as Mr Rosser – Rest his Soul! Stands to
reason he told your mum and having no call to
love your grandad neither she told you. I got to
thank you for not showing for all it don't surprise
me seeing you'll not want your grandad's dirty
washing hung out neither. And having heard from
more than <u>the One I will not name</u> you been good
to My Boy as thinks highly of you – I thank you
for it. <u>I will not name him neither</u>. He don't know
he's mine and <u>HE IS NOT TO KNOW NEVER</u>. I
swore on my Bible he would never hear it from me
on the night D.A.'s first lad come stillborn and
being cruel poorly with the childbed fever she
never knew she lost hers and got mine born the
night previous under the same roof. The Mistress
told her mine come stillborn and not to say and
seeing she and me been friendly when we was girls
down St Martin she never told none nor spoke of
it to me private – Rest her Soul! Your grandad
swore likewise he see My Boy was alright and I be

taken care of and I got to say he kept his word so I reckon Good Lord forgiven him for all I'll not NEVER.

D.A. always reckoned Mine the pick of her crop. She was a good Soul as deserved better than T. as had a bad side and knocked her about shocking and that troubles me now. I got to tell you I don't like the side I come to see in the One that got none of his bad blood. I don't know how he come by it but I see it clear for all he's ever so good lending me the hand and giving me a laugh and looking like butter not melt in his mouth. I don't like the company he been keeping and I don't know what to do for the best and it troubles me cruel. I don't like to put more on paper but I got to talk to you private Miss. I will be obliged if you would call when next passing my door.

I hope this finds you in good health.
Yours faithfully.
E. V. Mercer. Miss.

P.S. I just found I got no stamp and seeing Post Office be closed when I get up Coxden W.I. will post in morning.

I read the letter twice, mopped my eyes and handed it to David. 'D.A. and T. Dora and Ted Ames.'

He nodded and I watched the heightening tension in his downcast face as he read it twice: first rapidly, then slowly. Before he finished the first, I knew what to do. When he looked up his eyes were guarded. 'Convenient and simple solution in that time and place. Poor old girl.

She had all her marbles. But a stamp wouldn't have saved her.'

'I know. But it could've saved Murdo.'

'Possibly.' He looked down at the letter. 'Not being a lawyer, I can't be sure, but I suspect that as this was written within hours of her death, it could constitute a dying declaration.' He looked back at me. '*Ergo* – a query legal document.'

'Uh-huh. But no query that it is now my legal property.' I held out my hand and he gave it to me and watched deadpan as I tore it to shreds and shoved them back in the envelope. 'I'll burn this in the kitchen sink, later.' I glanced at my watch. 'I must ring Walt before he goes up to the Crown for his pint. Don't go. This won't take long.'

'Right.' He drew up a chair and sat facing me, wearing his most stolid expression.

Walt answered my call. 'Nah, not disturbing my tea, madam. I've had it.' The new bleak undercurrent in his slow voice was even more audible over the line than in person and it hurt my heart. 'What can I do for you, madam?'

'Can you spare a few minutes for a private talk?'

'Just hold on the tick, madam.' I heard him asking his wife to shut the door, then: 'Ready when you are, madam.'

'Thanks, Walt. I want to ask you to do me a tremendous favour and expect you'll want to think it over before discussing it with Mrs Walt. It's this – would you take over the whole estate for me for a few months and perhaps longer? Of course, if you will, you'll have a full-time secretary, sub-agent for the estate property, resident caretaker in this house – but we'll deal with the nuts and bolts later. Naturally the farm remains in your sole charge, but I do want you in overall charge of the rest. I know this means shoving an enormous amount of extra work on you, but if you will think it over and give me your decision when you're ready, I'll be enormously grateful.'

The brief silence was just long enough for David to hitch down his glasses. 'Aye. I'll take over for you, madam. Any time it suits. Thinking to take a long holiday, are you?'

'Not exactly.' I looked at David. 'I just hope that's how it'll turn out, but I wouldn't bet on it. Thing is, Walt – and you'll be the first I've told this – I want to marry Mr Lofthouse.'

'You don't say, madam!' For the first time in weeks I heard a smile in his voice. 'Mind you – if you'll pardon the liberty, madam – I can't say I've call to be surprised and can't put the name to one as has, after the years Mr Lofthouse been courting you being a real clever young gentleman as knows what he wants and how to wait for it. He's not far wrong there. He couldn't do better and I'll not say you're doing wrong, madam. He's all right. I wish you health and happiness and my wife'll say likewise once you give me leave to tell her.'

'Thanks a lot, Walt. It's no secret now you know, and I know you'll manage Endel while I'm away.'

'Much obliged, I'm sure, madam. Ta.' There was an old warmth and a new hint of pleasurable anticipation in his voice. 'I'll sort it for you and have the word with my wife. You'll tell Mr Lofthouse I wish him all the best? Right, then, madam. 'Evening.'

I put down the receiver and David stood up. 'Sure as

hell,' he said, coming round the desk to me and taking off his glasses, 'old Wenden knew your father, Rosie.'